IOWA'S DEVOTED DAUGHTER

Iowa's Devoted Daughter

THE STORY OF MISS HARRIET LOUISE ANKENY AND HER AMERICAN FAMILY

Karla Wright

ISBN-13: 9781533696410
ISBN-10: 1533696411
Library of Congress Control Number: 2016909658
CreateSpace Independent Publishing Platform
North Charleston, South Carolina

TABLE OF CONTENTS

INTRODUCTION

―――――∞∞∞――――――

THIS IS A STORY ABOUT the real life of Miss Harriet Louise Ankeny. [1] [2] She was born late to her parents and was raised like an only child. She was surrounded and nurtured by her older sisters and brothers and her mother and father. She was a precocious child, her father's delight and her mother's worry. She was sent to a female seminary (boarding school) as a teen-ager. After the Civil War, Harriet's whole family made Iowa their home. She grew into a woman with her own unique ambitions. Harriet's adventurous spirit propelled her to travel throughout America and the world. She lived and worked in Washington D.C. but returned to her family in Iowa. She enjoyed learning and travel but always longed to be home with her family. She lived with and cared for her parents until their deaths.

The story describes what life in America was like from 1844 to 1921 for an intelligent, adventurous and caring woman who called Iowa home. [3] The story also chronicles the lives of the whole Ankeny family. They were a real family – a prominent and prosperous family. The Ankeny family legacy of hard work, perseverance, loyalty, intelligence and continuous learning, along with their love of family and country, have made Iowa and America better places.

This book is a combination of storytelling and genealogy. The personalities and relationships in this story have been developed and embellished to create an entertaining story. The names, dates, titles, honors and places are real.

The following quote seems particularly poignant for the Ankeny family and my need to memorialize their legacy.

"A strong plant needs good seed.
A tall tree requires deep roots.
A future of promises for any people
rests upon a worthy past, worthily kept." [4]

The Family of Joseph and Harriet Susanna Giese Ankeny

John Fletcher Ankeny | Peter Dewalt Ankeny | Henry Giese Ankeny | Rollin Valentine Ankeny | Susan Fletcher Ankeny Barcroft | Rosina Bonnet Ankeny | Mary Ellen Ankeny Clark | Harriet Louise Ankeny

CHAPTER 1

TELL ME ABOUT MY GRANDFATHER AGAIN

———∞∞∞———

1854

THE ANKENY HOUSEHOLD IN MILLERSBURG, Ohio was always overflowing with family and friends. On this day Harriet Louise was running up and down the staircase, peeking in the cooking kitchen, staring at the festive dining table and looking out the front window for guests. A tenth birthday was always celebrated more than other birthdays in the Ankeny family. After Harriet Louise's sister, little Rosina Bonnet, died at seven years of age, Harriet Louise's mother felt like there would be no more birthday celebrations ever again in her home. Harriet Susanna mourned deeply when her fragile and beautiful daughter, named after her husband's mother, became ill in the middle of an exceptionally cold December, and could not regain strength and died on Christmas Eve. Harriet Susanna thought her childbearing days were over with four boys and three girls (two alive and one dead). When she discovered she might be having another child, she was stunned, surprised and concerned. Then she came to embrace the idea and the thought of a new baby pulled her out of her sullen state of mourning and back to life for herself and her large family.

So today, Harriet Susanna's final baby, Harriet Louise, was ten years old. There would be a party. Cakes, punch and tea would be served on the dining table that was still decorated in autumn like colors and decorations.

When Harriet Louise started rattling off exclamations of excitement about her wrapped presents, her mother scolded her and reminded her that such behavior was rude and presumptuous. Harriet Susanna taught all her

Rosina Bonnet Ankeny
1835 - 1842

children to display modesty and show appreciation for the material possessions they were privileged to enjoy. She reminded them that only hard work
and sacrifice led to delayed enjoyment of the finer things in life.

Joseph, unlike his wife Harriet Susanna, was much more outgoing and
boastful. He was definitely a man of much determination, courage and fortitude. With his youngest child, and he knew his last, he was very indulgent.
In fact he took pleasure in spoiling Harriet Louise. He was strict with his
first seven children, but with Harriet Louise, he let her get away with what
Harriet Susanna considered, embarrassing misbehavior.

When Harriet Louise exclaimed in front of the guests, "I am such a special little girl, look at all these presents, everyone loves me," her mother was
mortified. Her father just laughed and laughed and then said out loud for
everyone to hear "it's true." Harriet Susanna closed her eyes, slowly shook
her head back and forth, but a slight smile appeared on her face. It did seem
Harriet Louise had something special about her. Harriet Susanna did believe,
after all, that little Harriet Louise was God's gift to her, sent to mend her
very broken and grieving heart.

Harriet Louise Ankeny
Ten Years Old
1844 - 1921

Harriet Louise always had lots of friends at her home to help her play with her large doll collection. They pretended they were mothers themselves and sat on the floor with their tea cups and talked about growing flowers, having babies and voting for president. When the conversations were overheard by Harriet Susanna, she was quick to teach the girls that it was not lady like and not proper to talk about childbirth in public and that women, of course, did not vote, only men voted. She encouraged them to continue talking about growing flowers and gave them horticulture books from Joseph's library. Harriet Susanna steered little Harriet Louise into playing the piano and tending the flower gardens and orchards. Their Millersburg home had the only piano in the town. The piano and flower gardens were attractions for the childhood friends of little Harriet Louise. Harriet Louise had many privileges growing up in Millersburg. She had many friends and a large loving family. She had access to material possessions few others had. However, it was her companionship with her father, Joseph, and her desire to hear Joseph's stories, read his books, ride his horses, go to his men-only meetings that made little Harriet Louise the happiest.

So on the evening of her tenth birthday, after the party and the many presents were opened and displayed, Joseph asked little Harriet Louise, "if you could have anything you want today, what would it be?" Harriet did not hesitate a moment and replied, "please tell me again the story about your grandfather and father and how they sailed across the ocean and fought the Indians and lived in the woods."

So in the end it was not the material possessions that captivated little Harriet Louise's heart, it was the history of the Ankeny family. Joseph was more than willing to tell the stories again.

Harriet Louise's oldest sister Susan [5] looked really tired. She and her husband, Mr. John Barcroft, [6] said their good nights. Harriet Louise knew she was not supposed to talk about babies before they were born, but she also knew that Susan was going to have a baby and soon. Harriet Louise's brother Rollin, [7] his beautiful wife Sarah and their infant son Irvine also decided to call it a day and headed out to their own home.

Harriet Louise liked her first nephew, Irvine, well enough, but she was a little envious of him being the center of attention today. It was her birthday after all. His dreadful dirty diapers that required constant attention were distressing to little Harriet Louise. Harriet Louise tried to help clean out one of the disgusting nappies in the remote back bedroom. While there Harriet Louise witnessed her sister-in-law Sarah secretly nursing baby Irvine. Harriet Louise was startled at the sight of Irvine nursing and clinging to Sarah. The image of a little human being latching onto and sucking from another human being was a new, and actually alarming, vision for little Harriet Louise. Since Harriet Louise was the youngest child in the family, she did not witness her mother going through childbearing, birthing or nursing. Now, at ten, she was learning about womanhood from Sarah. Sarah sensed little Harriet's alarm. Sarah tried to comfort and reassure little Harriet and explained that someday she too would become a woman, get married, have a baby and share her life-giving breast milk. Little Harriet did not feel reassured. She did feel a closeness and special bond with her sister-in-law Sarah, more than with her own mother and sisters.

The Millersburg home was now quiet. Little Harriet and her sister, Mary Ellen, jumped up onto the davenport and sat on each side of Joseph. Mary Ellen was now fifteen years old and half girl and half woman. Tonight she was girl. The two daughters were eager to hear again the stories of adventurous, brave, loyal and patriotic men from their father. Joseph was eager to tell the stories about his father and grandfather. Joseph enjoyed being the center of attention in his home and in his community. He relished being the source of knowledge in all types of social circles and especially with his adoring family. Harriet Susanna with the help of Sassy quietly moved in and out of the parlor and dining room and cooking kitchen to pick up and wash dishes, store leftover food, stoke the fireplaces and ensure her daughters would hear and know their Ankeny heritage.

Joseph got comfortable. He unbuttoned his vest, stretched out his legs, and prepared himself for a long and enjoyable story-time with his two daughters. Joseph began.

Dewalt Ankeny   1746   Germany

"It all began with Dewalt Ankeny. [8] Dewalt is my grandfather. Dewalt was born in Germany. When Dewalt was only eighteen years old he came to the new world without his parents. You see his mother had lost six sons to war and she did not want her son, Dewalt, to die in war. She talked Dewalt's Uncle Casper into taking Dewalt with him to the new world. And so in 1746 they arrived, on a ship named Neptune, in the port of Philadelphia. This was well before the colonies fought for their independence. [9] [10] [11]

Dewalt was a busy man. He had three wives. He had twelve children. He also raised the father-less children of his third wife. He owned land in three places. Lancaster, Pennsylvania and Clear Springs, Maryland and Somerset, Pennsylvania. His Clear Springs home was his beloved abode. He developed orchards and built an impressive estate in Clear Springs. It is there he supplied, fed and housed soldiers during the Revolutionary War. [12] Grandfather

Dewalt is buried at Clear Springs where there is a beautiful monument honoring his life. [13] [14] [15]

Dewalt married Catherine. What happened to her no one knows. Dewalt then married your great grandmother, Mary Jane Domer. [16] They had a son named Peter Ankeny. Peter Ankeny is my father. They also had a son named Christian and three daughters, Anna Maria, Catherine and Rebecca. They owned land and farmed in Lancaster County, Pennsylvania. Your great grandmother died on that farm in a fire. One night she saw their barn on fire and she ran into the barn to rescue the animals. She was not only trying to save the animals, she was also desperate to save her family from financial ruin. The animals were food and money and their livelihood. Her five children witnessed her demise. My mother never knew, or at least she never told me, where Grandfather Dewalt was on the night of the fire. Another mystery, only God knows. [17]

Now, you girls understand why I am always preaching to you to be careful with your candles and lamps, now don't you? (The girls bobbed their heads up and down.)

Now Dewalt was a widower and had five little children to care for and much work to be done. Dewalt needed a helper, a wife. He met Margaretha Becker Frederick. She was a widow who had recently lost her husband. Margaretha and her deceased husband, Noah, had four children and one on the way.

You girls know what that means, don't you? (The girls bobbed their heads up and down.)

Poor, poor, Noah Frederick. Such a tragedy. I've told you this story before, but tonight you two girls are old enough to hear the whole story. Your mother won't like it that I'm telling you this, so I'll whisper. You see Mr. Frederick was out in his farm fields plowing and tending his crops with his two sons. Out of nowhere with no provocation or reason, a group of Indians attacked them. Mrs. Frederick and her two daughters heard the commotion and they ran and hid in the barn. The Indians left Noah to die and lie in the dirt under the hot sun. The Indians captured the two boys and took them away. The boys' bodies were never found so the town people decided the boys were being held as prisoners and work slaves.

Poor, poor, Margaretha. Such a tragedy. Margaretha was left with two little daughters to raise. A sad little baby boy was born after his father had been killed. Margaretha needed a helper, a husband.

So in Lancaster County, Pennsylvania the families of Dewalt Ankeny and Margaretha Frederick merged. Dewalt raised Margaretha's three surviving children as his own. And the family continued to grow! Dewalt and Margaretha had seven more children.

My favorite relative from that large family is Framy Shaff. She is Margaretha's granddaughter. And guess who she married? She married Dewalt's grandson, Henry Chorpenning! Although Framy is not direct kin, I found her to be the kindest to me. She told me that she named her second son, Joseph, after me. I believed her then, but now I guess since I was only one year old when her son Joseph was born, she was probably just humoring me. After all, who would name their child after a baby with soiled diapers?

You know I should write to Framy. Will you girls help me write a letter to her and tell her about our family? (The girls bobbed their heads up and down.)

And you girls remember, don't you, who Framy's father-in-law was? (The girls shook their heads back and forth.)

He was none other than the great explorer and Somerset pioneer John Chorpenning! He was a close friend of Father! They must have been good friends because John Chorpenning married father's sister, Anna Maria Ankeny. [18]

Peter Ankeny   1776   Somerset County, Pennsylvania

Those men were great adventurers and risk takers. They were intrigued by the unsettled and promising lands out west. They traveled westward to a place that is now known as Somerset, Pennsylvania. At the time the land was heavily wooded with clean streams full of fish and there was plentiful game to eat. They considered it their promised land. They intended to fell the trees, tame the land and bring their families to this promised land. The Indians had a different idea and often harassed them as they worked on creating and building structures for humans and fencing for animals. They started going out west in 1773 which was three years before the Revolution. Every winter they would return east to their families to the safety of the developed Frederick and Washington Counties. When the Colonies had succeeded in establishing their independence from England, about 1780, the Ankeny and Chorpenning families moved west and established permanent roots in Somerset, Pennsylvania. [19]

Your grandfather, Peter Ankeny, was the founder of Somerset. Someday I want you girls to see Ankeny Square in the middle of Somerset. Father and Mother made a prosperous and respectable life for themselves and their children. He left a farm to each of his ten children. Father donated land to the village for a school and churchyard. Your grandfather and grandmother, Peter and Rosina Bonnet Ankeny, are buried in Ankeny Square. [20] [21] [22]

I never knew my father. He died when I was only two years old. My many older brothers and sisters and step brothers and sisters and Mother told me many stories about his pioneering bravery, courage and determination, and allegiance, loyalty and patriotic service to the Colonies and the cause of freedom. I was born over fifty years ago but I remember the stories well.

Will you girls promise to remember these stories and pass them on to your children? (The girls bobbed their heads up and down.)

You girls must also always remember how your grandfather and great grandfather fought in and gave allegiance to the Colonies in 1776 when they fought a war for our independence and freedom from the dictatorial King of England. Father, like many men, served on the frontier in the county militia and he rose to the station of Captain. I was not even born when our country was born. I wish I could have fought in the Revolutionary War. My father worked hard to develop Somerset and he fought to keep it. [23]

I think I am a lot like my father. My father left his comfortable home in Maryland that his father created to go to western Pennsylvania. I left my comfortable home in Pennsylvania that my father created to go west, and here we are in Ohio.

And after seeing the bountiful and beautiful plains of Iowa this past summer, I know where my heart and next journey will take me. Your brothers already tell me that the land in Iowa is so fertile and the rivers so plentiful and plains so manageable that we must be part of this next great westward movement in America.

Sorry girls, I was day dreaming there for a moment about the future, now back to your ancestors. (The girls were sound asleep.)

So your great grandfather Dewalt Ankeny was laid to rest in Clear Springs, Maryland near his beloved farm and orchards. Your grandfather Peter Ankeny was laid to rest in Somerset, Pennsylvania in the village he founded and loved. I wonder, dear daughters, where your father's tired old body will be laid to rest."

Joseph looked to his left and to his right. His daughters' heads rested on his broad shoulders. They were sound asleep. He carefully slipped himself off the davenport, tenderly placed his sleeping daughters safely on the parlor davenport, picked up his shoes and tiptoed to the back remote bedroom where Harriet Susanna was already sound asleep.

CHAPTER 2

MY FATHER IS JOSEPH, THE FATHER OF JESUS

—— ∞∞ ——

1850's

ONE UNSEASONABLY WARM SUNDAY AFTERNOON in early December, Harriet Louise and her four girlfriends were playing with Harriet's many dolls, discussing babies, where babies come from, and the baby Jesus on the front porch of the Millersburg, Ohio home.

They tried to repeat and understand the words they heard that morning in Sunday School -- immaculate conception. They learned in Sunday School that Joseph was the father of Jesus. Harriet Louise then informed her friends with great authority that her father, Joseph, was the father of Jesus. They all believed it. After all, Joseph was the most respected and successful man in Millersburg, Ohio.

Harriet Louise adored her father. He never scolded her. He would allow his youngest child to ride horse back with him to his many men-only political meetings. When they came home smelling of cigar smoke, Harriet Susanna chastised them both. Little Harriet was most intrigued with the secret meetings her father attended -- the ones she was not allowed to attend. In her imagination she envisioned that it was at these meetings that the immaculate conception (whatever that was) occurred. Someday she vowed to herself she would find out what these secret meetings were all about.

Harriet Louise did know a lot about her father. She knew that Joseph was only two years old when his own father died. Harriet Louise mulled that over many times wondering what it would be like to not have her father. It made her love her father even more. When Harriet Louise was bored of her repetitious school assignments, she would beg to not go to school reminding her parents that Father left school when he was only thirteen. But there were things her father did that Harriet Louise knew about but wanted no part of, such as rafting down the flood swollen waters of the Ohio River while watching for Indians hiding in the dense forests.

Joseph was a story teller. He was also an educator and advisor to his sons. Harriet Louise listened and absorbed his conversations with his four sons. Joseph made sure his sons knew the hearty stock they came from. Joseph encouraged his sons to explore new frontiers like he did. Joseph had wanderlust in his veins. Joseph left home and visited his brother who had traveled west to Illinois as a teenager. When Joseph returned home to Pennsylvania his Uncle Colonel John Bonnet tried to settle him down and trained him as a storekeeper and businessman. Joseph said he was encouraged to settle down, to return to church, and to marry. Joseph attended a German Reformed church in Berlin, Pennsylvania. The missionary and pioneer minister was Reverend Henry Giese who came to America back in 1776. Joseph said he was impressed with the minister because he could sing, and preach, and play musical instruments and could create quite a stirring in his soul. Joseph would laugh and confess that really he was more impressed with his beautiful daughter, Harriet Susanna. Joseph insisted his sons find a good woman of equally fine family lines to share a family and livelihood and go to church. Harriet Louise loved to eavesdrop on the Ankeny men dining room table talk.

Harriet Susanna did not do a lot of story-telling but she delighted in telling about their very elaborate wedding in July of 1823 in Berlin, Pennsylvania. Sometimes Harriet Susanna would even bring out the bridal dress she wore -- a white silk gown trimmed with a lace ruff. Harriet Louise loved looking at the dress and dreamed of wearing it on her own wedding day. Joseph and Harriet Susanna then joined together and both shared the story about the extraordinary horseback ride back to Somerset after the ceremony, and how nine couples traveled with them the nine miles, and that they all continued celebrating the next day. They were always giddy when they told that story. Then Harriet Susanna would begin the boring inventory litany of all the fine linens, chairs, chests, bureaus and tables they received for wedding gifts which they still possessed and how they must be saved and preserved within the Ankeny family.

When Joseph and Harriet were first married they lived at the Ankeny homestead, staked by Dewalt and Peter, in Somerset where their four sons were born. Joseph's larger than life personality and desire for adventure led him to pack up his family and move westward. In 1831 they packed their belongings and four boys and left in the best equipped outfit that ever left Somerset County for Ohio where they put down roots in Holmes County. Joseph and Harriet soon became respected and prosperous citizens of Holmes County, Ohio.

Joseph Ankeny (1802-1876) Harriet Susanna Giese Ankeny (1801-1897)

Harriet Louise found and saved a printed program from 1834 when Joseph was sworn in as Legislator from Holmes County in the Ohio Legislature. It summarized her father's accomplishments: "Mr. Joseph Ankeny originates from Pennsylvania where he was commissioned by the Governor of Pennsylvania as Lieutenant Colonel of the Allegheny Jackson Legion of the State Militia. He was initiated into the Masonic fraternity in Somerset and continues membership in Ohio. Joseph mastered life's valuable lessons and became recognized as a man of keen insight into business situations early on where he managed a general store for his brother-in-law back in Pennsylvania. Mr. Ankeny is now a leading merchant in Holmes County, Ohio. He is a part owner of the flour mill. He possesses respected skills in farming, horticulture and orchards. He was commissioned a Brigadier General of the Ohio Militia, July 4, 1834 requiring the control of mustering and important events. His capable horse is also well known and respected and is known for standing fire without flinching."

Joseph was a prominent political and community figure. His affairs required their home to be the center of many meetings and special events and speeches. He was appointed postmaster of Millersburg in 1838 requiring even more meetings in their home. Joseph's activities in the Masonic fraternity were always conducted out in the country never at their home.

Joseph traveled to the East Coast on horseback and stage coach to New York, Baltimore, Philadelphia and New England factory towns to purchase goods for the Millersburg general store. Harriet Louise missed her father when he was gone but the celebratory homecomings were worth it.

Joseph and Harriet Susanna took the train to New York and visited the much talked about Crystal Palace, made of steel and glass, and established by P. T. Barnum for the World's Fair. The residents of the village of Millersburg were all amazed and impressed with their fancy travels to New York. Joseph and Harriet hosted an event at their home and Joseph told of their adventure. Joseph held everyone's attention with his story about the water closet. He explained how he had to pay a penny to use the contraption. Joseph declared that his family would soon have a retiring room in their home to house a water closet and the days of the outdoor privy would soon be history. Harriet Louise thought that was the best news. Harriet Susanna was totally embarrassed even contemplating the subject with mixed company. Harriet Susanna quickly changed the subject and insisted everyone have something to eat. Harriet Susanna with the help of Sassy provided refreshments. Joseph and Harriet were leaders in the social and business circles of Millersburg.

Harriet Louise was proud of her parents, of their Millersburg home, of their success, of their influence, and of their wealth. Harriet Louise loved being an Ankeny. [24] [25] [26] [27] [28] [29] [30] [31]

CHAPTER 3

OH BROTHER!

———— ✖ ————

"if Joseph wanted something for his sons, he always got his way"

CHRISTMAS CAME AND WENT. LIKE in past years, Harriet Susanna cried a lot around Christmas. Losing her daughter on Christmas Eve left her so sad that she could barely function. But somehow she did. She baked, she hosted family and friends at the home and she organized the church events. Three sons were living out west and did not return for Christmas. This was distressing to Harriet Susanna also. She waited in anticipation every day in December for a letter from John Fletcher or Peter Dewalt or Henry Giese. No letters arrived in December.

JOHN FLETCHER ANKENY
Finally the second week in January a letter arrived from California. Billy Wiggins was paid ten cents to hand deliver posts to residences in Millersburg. Harriet Louise saw Billy walking up to the porch and jumped up and down in anticipation of a letter from one of her brothers. She ran back to the cooking kitchen and told her mother, "Billy is coming!" They both opened the door before Billy could even knock. Billy handed Harriet Susanna the letter. It was from California and it looked like it had been around the world. And it had been. His letters from Sacramento left on a ship to central America, then crossed the narrow strip of land called Panama, and then was loaded

14

onto another ship to the Port of New Orleans and then up the Mississippi and Ohio Rivers and then over land on a dusty stage coach to Ohio.

John Fletcher wrote the letter on December 1. It read: Merry Christmas to my wonderful family! It does not feel like Christmas here. The weather is warm and beautiful. Sacramento is an exciting city. The California legislature is totally chaotic. I am trying to bring some order to this state, but it is frustrating. It is challenging being the very first legislative clerk in a brand new and untamed state. My practice is taking a lot of my time too. Too many women having babies and too many contagious diseases. I can treat those conditions. I can treat the many gun shot and knife wounds. But I can't help the many people who succumb to the most awful types of human conditions where their bodies waste away and life fades from them. I learned many medical techniques from Dr. Voorhees and Dr. McNeal and at the medical college in Cincinnati, but there is so much more that I do not know -- that I know. I really feel these days that I miss the plains of Ohio and I miss my family. Medicine is a noble profession, but I really feel these days that my calling is not with people's miseries. I really feel I need to be involved with the development of the land and communities and enterprises. When I bring order to land ownership or village rules, I really feel I can help people more to create for them a stable and safe home and livelihoods. I have trained a very able assistant here to perform many of the medical procedures and some days I do not even have to go to a home or infirmary or jail to treat an ailing subject. She can perform the tasks as well as I can. It takes more thoughtful resolve to build a village with transportation lanes and commerce. Those are my musings for this December. I hope this letter finds you all well and happy and joyous for the celebration of Christ's birth! Dear Mother, please find peace and happiness. Dear Sisters, help your Mother and love your Father. Please write me and tell me about life in Illinois and Ohio and the new excursion you made into Iowa. Your description of Iowa from your trip there last summer sounds like it is a wonderful place with plentiful opportunities for commerce and agriculture. I am restless out here in California and yearn to be back in Ohio but I will fulfill my obligations to the people here. Your loving son and brother, J. F.A. P.S. I will tell you all about my voyage to the

Hawaiian Islands when I see you. There is just too much to describe in a letter, I will have to tell you in person. [32] [33]

Harriet Louise and her mother read the letter together and then they read it again, and again. Harriet Susanna shed tears of joy to hear from her oldest son. They both were buoyed by the even remotest thought that maybe, just maybe, John Fletcher Ankeny, would return to Ohio to see them all soon.

Joseph read the letter when he returned to his home shortly before dark. He was less than pleased with John Fletcher's outpouring of emotion and carrying on about his work and his desire for his own happiness over his responsibilities. Joseph said nothing after reading the letter. Joseph did, however, begin thinking if John Fletcher were to return, he needed to go to Iowa. That is where the next "promise land" was for the Ankeny family. If Joseph wanted something for his sons, he always got his way.

The very next day Billy Wiggins was walking up to the house again. This was too good to be true. Harriet Susanna was not at home. She and some town ladies were at the school building cleaning and preparing materials and training the new school teacher. School would start back up soon for Harriet Louise and Billy Wiggins. Today though Harriet was happy to see Billy again not only to receive another letter but to get a chance to talk to Billy. Uncertain why she liked seeing Billy so much, she did though. Billy was a good looking teen-ager. Four or five years older than Harriet Louise. He was smart in school. He was well mannered too. And he already had a job as a post carrier. He was ambitious. Harriet had been thinking beforehand a topic of conversation when she saw Billy again. Harriet asked Billy, "how do you like your job as post carrier?" Billy responded, "I really like it. When I deliver posts to people they are very happy to see me. They are happy and I am happy." Harriet Louise thought that was just the best answer. Billy was a carefree and happy spirit and always smiling. Billy tipped his hat to Harriet and said, "well have a nice day." Harriet took the posts and went inside and thought I can't wait for school to start and I will get to see Billy every day.

PETER DEWALT ANKENY

A very short letter from brother Peter Dewalt Ankeny was sent from Iowa. It read: To my very dear family, I apologize for not greeting you at Christmas time. Here in Iowa we had a dreadful blizzard and I was stuck in a boarding house for over a week. Dear Father, the land we looked over last summer appears to be available for our purchase. It is near a very small village called Berwick. It already has a postal station which is helpful. I don't have a good place to live yet and am working on that. I am busy from daylight to twilight. Our two grand horses and the buckboard wagon are holding up well for me to get around for necessary provisions. My law studies have come in handy for processing all of the necessary paperwork for land ownership here. I feel I am a step ahead of everyone else. Also my two colleagues from the Mexican War are helpful to me for navigating the transportation road and river ways in Iowa. Fort Des Moines is helpful to the new land owners here. Believe it or not, the Indians still live near here, and sometimes cause trouble. We are not the only ones seeking homes here. Last year's drought out east brought many people, some say 150,000 people, to Iowa. So Dear Father, the time is now to act and buy land for farms and orchards and enterprises. Dear sweet Mother, I am sorry I did not see you on Christmas Eve. I know how hard it is for you. I thought of you and said a prayer for you and for my little sweet and gentle sister, Rosina Bonnet, who plays now in heaven with our Lord. Your loving son and brother, Peter. [34] [35] [36]

Harriet Louise was so happy because she knew when her mother and father returned home they would be ecstatic with joy for having two letters in two days from her much loved older brothers.

And she was right, they were glad to hear from Peter. But they were unsatisfied that they had not heard from Henry Giese for many months.

HENRY GIESE ANKENY

Joseph fumed about Henry not writing from California. Henry was head strong and left for California five years ago in 1850 when the gold excitement was high. Of course Joseph and Harriet Susanna understood the difficulty of getting messages back and forth from remote places in California. Harriet Susanna said "now if only we would hear from Henry, life would be good. We don't even know if he is alive or dead." Joseph bristled at his wife and insisted she never say those words again. "We must always think positive. We must always believe in our sons. They are strong and intelligent men and don't need to be worried about or pampered." Harriet Susanna just turned away and went into the cooking kitchen and began doing meal preparation chores. Harriet Louise knew to stay quiet and she set the table for the four of them. Mother, Father, Harriet and Mary Ellen. [37] [38]

The long dining room table seemed extra huge when it was just the four of them. Their older sister Susan and her husband often stopped in and shared an evening meal with them. Susan helped her husband at his law office during the day and so they welcomed a meal made by Harriet Susanna. But that happened less and less during these winter months and also because Susan was about to have a baby any day now it seemed. She often stayed home and did not go to the law office. Harriet Louise, in fact, sometimes went to Mr. Barcroft's law office and did recordkeeping and filing. Harriet's penmanship and vocabulary were exceptional and very useful in a law practice. Harriet enjoyed penning in property plats and legal explanations. She also was good at proofing wills and she actually enjoyed reading them for their entertainment value as much as proofreading them for correct grammar. Harriet told her father one evening during the evening meal that she would probably start working for Mr. Barcroft full time when the baby arrives and she would become an attorney soon. Joseph and Harriet Susanna both about dropped their eating utensils at the same time at such an idea. They smiled at each other and Joseph said, "only from this one's mouth would such a preposterous idea come." Harriet Susanna shut her eyes, shook her head from side to side slight and smiled a slight smile. An expression Harriet Louise had come to know well.

ROLLIN VALENTINE ANKENY

Later in the evening Rollin Valentine stopped by to read the letters from his two brothers John Fletcher and Peter Dewalt. [39] [40] [41] When Harriet Louise disappointedly saw that Sarah had not accompanied her husband, she went on up to her bedroom to prepare for the next day at school. She pondered which pinafore to wear and wondered which one might draw the attention of Billy Wiggins. She asked her sister, Mary Ellen, if she liked Billy. Mary Ellen said she liked him okay. He was polite and smart. She said, no I mean REALLY like him, like in boy friend girl friend. Mary Ellen acted as if a dirty word had been spoken and said, of course not. Harriet Louise thought, good.

The last few days had been full of thoughts of men. She thought about her brothers who lived out west in unknown lands. Billy Wiggins became a person who consumed Harriet's imagination. Father was becoming more and more stern it seemed. Harriet Louise idolized Mr. Barcroft and she thought she might want to be just like him when she grew up. Tomorrow she would meet her new teacher named Mr. Lincoln.

CHAPTER 4

HARRIET LOUISE GROWS UP

———— ⌘ ————

SCHOOL WAS OUT FOR THE summer. Mary Ellen finished all the learning available to her at the Millersburg school. When walking home on the last day, Mary Ellen, now 16, and Harriet Louise, 10, were seriously and secretly talking about the school teacher, Mr. Lincoln, and how handsome he was and how they were going to miss him. They also talked about Billy Wiggins and how he was the most popular boy in town. Mary Ellen said she might try to flirt with him and become his wife. Harriet Louise was upset and jealous about that. Harriet Louise had her eyes on Billy for a long time, but Billy was, after all, Mary Ellen's age. Harriet Louise said she heard that Billy as going to move to Iowa anyway so Mary Ellen might as well get over him now. Mary Ellen quietly agreed. Then Mary Ellen went into one of her very, very quiet and sedentary stages. When she got home she went to their bedroom and stayed there for the next three days. She claimed she was sick, but Harriet Louise knew she was not really ill. She was not vomiting, she did not have a fever, she was reading books and embroidering pillow cases for her hope chest. However, Harriet Louise was worried about these bedroom spells. She found traces of blood in the chamber pot which Mary Ellen would use because she did not or could not walk outdoors to the privy. Mother came and went into their room and brought in food and items and removed dirty laundry and washed them immediately. So Harriet finally just jumped on the bed and got in Mary Ellen's face and said, "Are you really sick? You don't seem sick. You are not going to die like Rosina are you?" Mary Ellen put down her needle and thread and said, "It is time you know. You see,

Harriet, when we grow up, we become women and we have to go through changes every month so that we can have children. You know where babies come from don't you?" Harriet Louise was now totally enthralled with this revelation. Mary Ellen continued, "Mother explained it to me the first time the monthly discharge of blood happened. I thought I was going to die like sister, Rosina. But Mother said that it was a natural act of God and it was proof that God loved me and would prepare me to have children to love also. So when I get this discharge it soaks through my clothes so I can't go out in public or to school. Mother helps me. Mother will help you when your time comes." Now Harriet Louise was mortified. She wanted no part of bleeding. She was pretty sure now that she wanted no part of childbirth either. Her imagination was going wild. Then she stopped and thought about Billy. Maybe she did want to have a baby and Billy would be the father and they would be married and run the postal station together. But Harriet would have to grow up a lot more before that could happen. In the meantime, Harriet thought she best stay away from kissing anyone for fear a baby would develop in her stomach like Irvine grew in Sarah's stomach and like Mary Louise grew inside Susan's stomach.

Soon Mary Ellen was up and around again, just like before. There was a lot of talk about the Cleveland, Ohio Female Seminary. [42] Mary Ellen would be going there to advance her education so that she would be worthy of a husband and be able to create a beautiful and large family. Harriet Louise was forlorn about the possibility of her being the only child left in the large Ankeny home and was sincerely sad to know that Mary Ellen would not be there for her to share secrets and talk about babies and kissing.

Mary Ellen packed bags and books and supplies and left with Joseph in the horse drawn carriage to Cleveland, Ohio. Soon school would be starting up again for Harriet Louise but she had two weeks before she would have to study so she gathered up her friends and they played house and had tea parties and laughed on the front porch. Sometimes they discussed babies and Harriet Louise told them about Mary Ellen's description of womanhood. Some of Harriet's friends said they already knew about that curse first hand. Harriet was growing up and fast.

Harriet was a little bored with the tea parties and dolls and was contemplating a bigger adventure with her friends. Harriet's father attended secret meetings. So secret that Harriet was not allowed to go with Joseph. Often Joseph took Harriet with him to city meetings, political talks, and business negotiations. They rode on horseback to and from the orchards and took notes and talked about the produce, the insects, the need for rain. Harriet was her father's best record keeper of the farm and orchard production, planting and sales. But Harriet was not satisfied until she knew what the secret meeting was about. So Harriet convinced her friends one evening to walk a long three miles out to the Masonic Lodge. It was a big grand log building in the woods. Many horses were tied up outside the lodge which meant there were lots of men in the building. Harriet and her friends tiptoed to the windows and looked into the large room where men were talking, smoking cigars and pipes. There was a large carved sign that said "Spartan Lodge, A. F. & A. M., Millersburg, Ohio". She saw her father standing in front of the men and he had a large wooden medallion with the word Warden hung from his neck. She watched him talk to the men but she could not hear what they were saying. Then something spooked the horses and they began to snort and make noise. The men looked startled and frightened. They rose up and drew their side arms and pointed them toward the doors. Joseph then spotted his own daughter's face looking in the window. He bellowed out, "don't shoot!" Joseph opened the door and saw four terrified little girls looking up at him. He was very angry. He scolded Harriet in front of her friends for disobeying him. He then sat on the front step, hastily slung Harriet over his knees and swatted her three times on the behind and hard.

Harriet Louise was mortified. She was scared. She was embarrassed that her father had humiliated her in front of her friends. Then he threatened to tell the parents of her friends how disrespectful they were. He said, "stay here." He returned to the smoke filled room of men and sheepishly said, "I have to take my daughter and her friends home." He walked his horse home with the four girls trailing behind.

Harriet Louise came to the conclusion that night that her father, Joseph, was not after all the father of Jesus. The father of Jesus would never hit his child.

Usually it was mother who disciplined Harriet when she stepped out of line, but this time, Harriet Susanna was silent as Joseph continued to scold Harriet Louise when they were home. Harriet Louise was silent as well. She went to her room, she did not want to go to school and face her friends. She looked at the chamber pot in the corner and cried. She knew she was not going to be a little girl much longer.

CHAPTER 5

JOSEPHINE

—∞∞∞—

October 1855 Somerset, Pennsylvania

"two girls with very different backgrounds with stories to share"

IT WAS THE MIDDLE OF October and perfect weather for traveling far distances in the horse and carriage. No spring rains, no snow, and the roads were passable. Weather was cool enough that food did not spoil in the knapsacks. Animals did not require as much water to drink. If required, one could actually sleep in the carriage under blankets without mosquitoes attacking.

And so when the letter came from Pennsylvania saying that Framy Shaff Chorpenning had passed away, Joseph immediately made the decision that he, Harriet Susanna and Harriet Louise would go to Pennsylvania to pay respects to the grieving family. [43] It also meant that Harriet Susanna would see her Giese family and friends in Somerset and that lifted her spirits enormously.

Joseph chose two of his best horses to pull the newly acquired carriage. They packed trunks full of clothing and supplies and food and placed in the carriage. Harriet Susanna tried to convince Joseph that they should pay for and take a stage coach and leave the hard work of managing a team of horses to others. Joseph said he wanted the independence of managing his own time on this trip back to Pennsylvania. He did not want to be confined to others' schedules. Joseph of course carried firearms to protect his family against Indians, robbers and wild animals.

Harriet Louise was excited for this adventure. She needed some excitement and new experiences. She wanted to know more about Pennsylvania. She wanted to see where her father was born and raised and where her four brothers had been born. She wanted to meet cousins. She always wanted to meet Framy Shaff Chorpenning but, of course, she was now gone. She felt like she knew her though from her many letters. Harriet Louise was the most eager though to meet Framy's granddaughter, Josephine.

Framy and Joseph had encouraged the two girls to write to each other. Harriet had received only one, but very special, letter from Josephine. The handwriting was very hard to read and had many misspellings but the topics were understood. She wrote about hunting, roasting and eating turkey, making pillows from duck and geese feathers, and growing, pickling and eating green beans. Harriet Louise wrote several letters to Josephine and told about her doll collection, the very nice school teacher, and their orchards. In Harriet's last letter to Josephine, Harriet Louise used her imagination and told a story about how she and her friends had raided a secret meeting about a government revolution and they had been caught and punished severely but never cried during the punishment. It was half true. Now these two friends would actually meet and their real lives and stories would be known and cherished forever -- two girls with very different backgrounds with stories to share.

The trip was fun. They stayed in nice inns two nights and traveled slowly on the recently completed roadways. They ate the food they packed but also had interesting meals twice at new taverns along the new roadway.

Their first stop was at Samuel's Lutheran Cemetery outside of Lavansville, Pennsylvania to pay respect to Framy. [44] It was easy to find her resting place because the grass had not grown over the freshly dug soil. They placed wild flowers from the ditches upon the grave. Joseph said a prayer: "Oh come, Sweet Jesus, quickly come, And ease my aching breast, I long to reach my Heavenly home, To be with Christ is best." [45]

The three quickly made their way to Framy's home to see her husband, Henry Chorpenning. Henry was the son of John Chorpenning the famous Somerset explorer. It was John and Peter Ankeny who explored the untamed

Somerset County and built the churches, schools, commerce and homes there. When the Ankeny family arrived, the Chorpenning family was surprised to see them. Joseph and family had traveled faster in their own two horse carriage than the post could deliver a letter telling them they were on their way.

Henry was very happy to see them. Harriet Louise was beyond joyous to witness the hugging of grown men, something she did not see in Ohio, where handshakes were for men and hugging was for women. Many adults and children were at the home and they quickly rode their horses to tell other family members that the Ankenys of Ohio were in Pennsylvania. Harriet Louise eagerly awaited the arrival of Josephine.

It was late afternoon when a group walked up to the house. Harriet knew Josephine immediately. They were almost the same size. Harriet was boisterous and happy and Josephine was a little shy and didn't say much. But Harriet put an end to that quickly by whisking Josephine away from the loud crowd and asking her all kinds of questions about making pillows, and did she actually fire a gun, and how many green beans can she eat at one time.

Josephine proudly responded and told how she preserves the green beans by pickling them in a brine so they can eat them all winter. Harriet thought Josephine was the smartest girl she ever knew.

Harriet told Josephine that Josephine's uncle, Joseph, was named after her father, Joseph. Josephine told Harriet how she herself was named after her uncle, Joseph. Then Josephine really opened up and said, "You know my great great grandfather was Noah, don't you?" Harriet thought how wonderful to be related to Noah from the Bible. Josephine said, "He was killed by Indians and the Indians kidnapped his two sons but one of them came back." Harriet thought she could not compete with the great and adventurous stories of Josephine. Josephine went on, "The Shawnee Indians killed Noah while he and his two sons were working in the fields. They kidnapped the boys. They gave Thomas an Indian name, Kee-Saw-So-So and they pierced his ears. Many years later Thomas showed up and nobody recognized him, but his mother did. She knew him because he had a large scar on the back of his neck. Thomas could not speak very clear and when asked about his brother he always just cried like a little boy. But he became a man of great courage and he fought in our country's war for independence in 1776. He is a real hero." [46]

Harriet was transfixed with this story. She did not know of anyone who had actually been killed by an Indian, although she had heard plenty of stories. And now to learn about a kidnapping, an escape and a war hero all wrapped up into one story, it was captivating.

Harriet was always looking for the next adventure. She pondered for a moment how wonderful it would be to be kidnapped and then return and everyone would be so glad to see her. She thought more about that, leaving behind her family, going off to an unknown place, and then relishing the return. She really liked the idea of returning from a trip and telling everyone about her adventure. Harriet Louise loved homecomings.

Then Josephine and Harriet returned to the big family group and ate pickled beans and turkey. There was plenty of very salty fish, but it was tasty. There was bread and berry jams. A new vegetable called squash was served and Harriet liked it. Someone brought a bushel basket of new apples and everyone had their own apple. The children drank milk from their milking herds and the adults drank a dark brew from large jugs that came from an underground storage cellar. Then large ripe watermelons were cracked open and everyone laughed and ate and spit seeds everywhere. They ate outside so no one worried about table cloths, or silver, or napkins, or salt cups, like at home in Ohio. There were not enough tables and chairs so most everyone sat on the ground. Harriet always had a big appetite and was often hungry and never got enough to eat it seemed, but this night she was stuffed.

The autumn night air turned very cool very fast. Everyone went back home. The three travelers slept inside and were thankful because this night it got downright cold outside. Josephine spent the night with Harriet at her grandfather Henry Chorpenning's home. The girls slept on the floor on top of and under comforters soft with goose and duck down feathers. They whispered about their pets, their many dogs and cats, and their many funny names. They told stories about funny things their pets did, each trying to top the other's tale. Then they talked about growing up and having babies.

Harriet said she had a boyfriend named Billy. Josephine was impressed but warned her not to kiss him. Harriet was impressed with how smart Josephine was. Then they talked about moving out west to Iowa. Harriet said that her father had been to Iowa and he loves Iowa and her one brother, Peter, is already there. Josephine said her father knows some people who went to Iowa. Josephine confessed that she knew an older boy who was the same age as Harriet and she wants him to be her husband and his name is David Austin Barron and he was born just one month after Harriet Louise back in 1844. [47] Josephine said she hoped Harriet would meet David if we all go to church together on Sunday. Josephine explained that David's great great grandfather, named Nicholas, came from Germany and he built the church and school next to the cemetery where Grandmother Framy is buried [48] at the Samuel's Church. [49]

Harriet Louise was filled with wonder that Josephine was related to Noah of the Arc and was now somehow, some way, connected to Saint Nicholas of the Christmas celebration story fame. Harriet Louise had decided some time ago that her father was not the father of Jesus after all, after that humiliating spanking she received at the Masonic Lodge. She was still sorting out a lot of conflicting information about Jesus, the Holy Spirit and God. Maybe a Sunday worship service at the Samuel's Church of Lavansville, Somerset County, Pennsylvania would help.

Harriet thought about Mary Ellen and felt sorry that she was not with them enjoying this rich family reunion experience. Poor Mary Ellen she was probably at the dormitory at the female seminary reading books and laying in bed waiting for her monthly curse to end. Mary Ellen seemed so far away, so distant, so unknown right now. It seemed, on the other hand, that Harriet had known Josephine her whole life. They were so different yet so similar. Not really close kin but bonded by kindred spirits. Joseph called Josephine and Harriet shirt tail cousins.

Harriet Louise decided kindred spirit relationships mattered as much as close kin relations. Harriet concluded that special relationships were made as well as inherited.

The family stayed in Pennsylvania for three nights. They visited the Giese family, they attended a beautiful brick church in the country where many of their loved ones were buried. Harriet and Josephine were inseparable. But the day came when they had to say good bye. Harriet said write me more letters and I will write you too. Josephine agreed. Harriet said we will be pen pals! Josephine knew it wouldn't happen since she barely knew how to read or write.

CHAPTER 6

NEW YORK

—⊷∞∞⊷—

1858

"her father was a mortal man, with greatness and flaws"

BY THE END OF THE school year, Harriet Louise was the most advanced student in Millersburg. Mr. Lincoln the school master told Joseph and Harriet Susanna that he had taught Harriet Louise everything he could. She needed to go to a girls' seminary where she could get a more detailed education in science, history, geography and language arts. Joseph agreed that it was time for Harriet to leave the nest. It was past time in fact. Harriet was always one step ahead of her age group, investigating too much, wondering about things only adults thought about, asking too many questions. So Harriet Susanna and Joseph agreed. They also agreed that unlike her sisters before her, she would go out East to the best girls' seminary. The Hudson School for Girls in New York City. They had heard about this fine institution and its founders when they were in New York City in 1854. Money was no object. Tuition and room and board were expensive but the Ankenys were wealthy. Joseph was less concerned with Harriet learning about science and geography and more concerned about her having some discipline and structure and learning an appreciation for the role of women in society and importance of motherhood.

So the day came. Harriet was told. Harriet was dismayed at first. How would she travel out there? Joseph assured her that the stage coach lines were safe and efficient now. And the trains were improving and increasing their stations all across America. She could travel by herself with paperwork and tickets and with no problem. Harriet seemed older than fourteen, but she was only fourteen.

Harriet had perfected the art of being a mature woman now. She learned how to care for her body and all her personal hygiene and grooming needs. She wore her hair pulled back and piled on top which required little or no fussing. She wore practical clothing most of the time. She refused to let being a lady hold her back. She did like dressing in her finest, sporting a fashionable hat preferably with feathers and jewelry when she and Billy would be together.

She lamented that she would be away from Billy. They saw each other every Sunday afternoon after church. They went on picnics together where they ate their lunch in the village park or in her backyard or in the orchards. In the winter they would go inside the new postal station to eat and talk. They would take their ice skates and glide across the creek and ponds. She sometimes would fall down on purpose so that he could help her up. Billy would take off his knitted cap and put it on Harriet's head to keep her warm. It was a gesture he often did, in some way representing that he wanted to take care of her. It gave her a thrill but she never ever, never in a million years, kissed him.

When she told Billy she was leaving for one or maybe two years, Billy was visibly saddened. Harriet asked him, "Billy, will you wait for me?" William Wiggins agreed.

It was unheard of for a girl of fourteen to cross Ohio to New York by herself, but Harriet Louise Ankeny was not your normal fourteen year old girl. Her father said she was fourteen going on twenty-four and had more wits about her than any of his sons. And after all, they had gone off to California during the gold rush and had already moved out to Iowa and Illinois.

Harriet arrived at the Hudson School with her three massive trunks of clothing, supplies and a few dolls. She was welcomed by the school superintendent and a select group of three girls who would become part of her four-member roommates. Conversations were flying every direction from where are you from? what is your favorite song? to what does your father do? and do you have a boyfriend?

The food was so delicious and so much better than home. Different, more spices and flavors, many more sweets. Fewer seasonal fruits but seafood was new and delicious.

Harriet prospered in her new environment. She loved learning from her beautiful new textbooks and the teachers were very smart and sophisticated. The maps of the world were hung on rods and could be pulled down and were the size of her bedroom walls at home. She studied and stared at those maps. Europe, Asia, Africa. She pondered going to Germany where the Ankeny family originated. London, Paris, Rome. Someday.

She loved learning how to read music and her piano playing excelled. She was the best pianist by far, but of course she had grown up with a piano in her home. She was not that good at singing, and was always criticized for her inability to keep in tune. But she loved singing anyway. And dancing, she learned waltz steps. Twice a year the female seminary held a very closely supervised dance with the local all-male school. There they perfected their dance steps so that when they were old enough to go to a real dance they would be ready. Harriet loved dancing and music.

The four dormitory girls bonded. She was lucky to have girls who were fun and interesting. These girls were so much more fun that her two sisters back home who seemed to have life itself sucked and drained out of them.

Harriet learned from her roommates and in biology class about how life was created. That was a shock to Harriet, but also a relief to know that when she returned home for Christmas she could let Billy kiss her and not end up with a baby in her stomach.

Harriet wrote to her parents and to Josephine often. Her mother wrote often and gave very descriptive accounts of the parties she hosted and town festivities she organized and her work with the local horticulture club. Josephine never wrote back but she did send a post card once. Joseph wrote letters with lists of responsibilities for Harriet and reminders to study hard and not waste food, money or time. Her brothers seemed to have totally forgotten about her. Rollin's wife, Sarah, of course, wrote to her. She wrote about little Harriet

Louise, now two years old, and how much she was growing and learning and the funny things she did. Sarah and Rollin named their second child Harriet Louise. And Harriet Louise could not have been more proud. Harriet Louise would be baby Harriet's Godmother. Sarah wrote about the dogs and cats and events in the town and what flowers and trees were blooming and changing. Sarah knew how to touch Harriet's heart with exactly what she was wondering about from back home in Millersburg. When Harriet dreamed of being Billy's wife, she envisioned herself to be just like Sarah.

In school there was a class called Civics. The teacher was an older man, always dressed in a three piece suit and tie. He knew, it seemed, about everything. He talked about how government worked in Washington, D.C., and in New York state. He seemed to think Ohio was in the wild west with no means of communication. But he did understand the important philosophies of slavery, of human rights and the importance of the U.S. Constitution and Bill of Rights.

He gave himself the title of abolitionist. He gave talks around New York about the sin of slavery. He did not believe any man can be owned by another man. Most people agreed with that, but then he said all slaves in the southern states must be freed immediately. Then people argued against that notion, wondering what would become of these people. Who would feed them? Where would they work? Where would they live? The many contradictory issues surrounding slavery made Harriet think about the meaning of life at a whole new and higher level. She loved hearing his lectures. He seemed like a preacher. He was very persuasive.

When Harriet returned home at Christmas she repeated her abolitionist lecturer theories and concerns and Joseph hit the roof. Joseph was not in favor of slavery at all, but he did not believe in disrupting others' rights and property and their freedom to own slaves if they thought it was best for their families and livelihoods. He would not own slaves, but he did not believe in abolishing slavery. And he sure as heck did not believe in going to war about it. And there was increasing talk about the southern states seceding from the United States and that the north would not allow it. They would fight a war to keep the union together.

Harriet saw Billy at Christmas time and they discussed the possibility of a war. Billy said he was ready to fight if it meant freeing the slaves. Harriet was in love.

Harriet returned to New York with the warning from her father to keep an open mind and to challenge the thinking of those highfalutin East coast academics. Harriet agreed to do just that. Harriet would keep an open mind. Her open mind found her going to meetings where the Grimke sisters [50] were talking about abolition and also women's rights to vote in elections. Harriet was developing into a tremendous vessel of knowledge and wisdom. Harriet knew better than to bring the voting rights subject up with her father though. She would have to plan a strategy for that conversation. But it did not matter. She now understood her father was a mortal man, with greatness and flaws. She understood her mother was a reflection of a time in history. She respected and loved her parents, but she no longer worshipped them. She loved and respected her four older brothers, but they really seemed like they didn't know she existed. And her two sad sisters she loved too, but they were as distant to her as her brothers. Sarah was not her blood relation but she seemed closest to Sarah. Sarah named her daughter after Harriet Louise. That meant so much. Just like Joseph had said that Framy Shaff Chorpenning was not close blood relation, she seemed the kindest to Joseph and she named her son after Joseph. The bonding of the human spirit is not always absolute with a parent and child, with a brother and sister. Bonding requires more than blood, it requires the desire to know and understand the other person, to care enough to spend time with and mentor another, and, yes, even give a new baby your name. Kindness and kindred spirit were more important than kin.

Harriet thought, if I do ever have a child with Billy, I will treat the baby as a human being not as my child as in ownership of property. No human being should or can own another human being.

In American literature class, Harriet was assigned the book "Uncle Tom's Cabin" to read and report. Harriet loved that the author shared her name. [51] Harriet was tasked with not only reading and reporting on a speech "Ain't I a Woman?" but also to analyze its content and prepare a statement of agreement or disagreement. Harriet loved that the speech was delivered in her home state of Ohio. Harriet was surprised that the orator was a former slave. [52]

In Civics class, Harriet heard debates about why women should not own property and why women should not be allowed to speak in public. Discussions about the economics and morality of slavery became more prevalent than women's rights in class. Harriet shared the letter she received from her oldest brother, John Fletcher, from California with the class and her teacher. John wrote to Harriet about how he worked for the inclusion of women as legal property owners in California and that California was the first state in the union to extend property rights to women. Harriet was pretty sure that was a good thing. Her father, Joseph, was mortified. Her Civics Professor was amazed and very impressed and he called upon Harriet more frequently in class after that revelation.

In Mathematics class, Harriet struggled with learning abstract formulas that seemed to have no purpose. She did enjoy keeping records and bookkeeping. Her days of working in Mr. Barcroft's law practice and keeping detailed planting and harvesting records for her father and her perfect hand writing all helped her achieve passing grades in Mathematics.

Harriet could not get enough of World History class. The textbook and maps were mesmerizing. She made up stories that included herself in these faraway places. She thought, if my great grandfather, Dewalt Ankeny, could sail across the ocean when he was only eighteen, then surely I can travel on a much safer steam ship to Germany and England and Africa and even China.

In Science class, Harriet learned enough to be disciplined in her understanding of nature and horticulture, life and reproduction, health and diseases. She would always trust that God was the creator of heaven and earth but she now would accept that the way the world was created could be explained by science as well as the Bible stories.

In Religion class, Harriet revered the Lord and accepted the Bible as truth, most of the time. But she often was deeply troubled with why God let people die because death caused so much heartache. She was growing increasingly concerned with all this war talk. Her vision of a bloody battle being fought by men she knew and loved and who might die kept her awake at night sometimes. The more she learned about abuses of people because of their race or their sex, the more she questioned why God would let that happen. But she kept her faith in God because to let go of her faith would mean she would have no peace at all.

When the weather was cold in New York she bundled up in her sophisticated, purchased wool coat and colorful, handmade scarves and the less than glamorous knitted cap that Billy had put on her head when they went ice skating back in Ohio. She and her roommates went on excursions into New York City with chaperones. She experienced museums and plays and concerts. She saw mammoth buildings that reached into the sky. Her Civics teacher called them Sky Scrapers. They visited the Crystal Palace. When Harriet told her friends that her parents traveled from Ohio to New York to attend the World Exhibition and Fair and see the Crystal Palace, the girls were never more impressed with Harriet and her family's status. They all paid a penny to use the newest flushing water closet in the retiring room.

The girls were taken on a field trip to a manufacturing facility where women sat or stood at machines to weave, cut and sew fabric into goods for purchase. The girls were Harriet's age and Harriet thought how stifling it would be to sit there for twelve hours all day and do the same thing over and over and over and over again. Harriet wondered if her father had witnessed these oppressive mass production factories on his East coast buying trips. She pondered that there must be a better way to produce goods without subjecting workers to boring and routine tasks.

Her last semester at the Hudson Seminary, the spring of 1860, was consumed with the talk of slavery, abolition, states' rights, a westerner named Lincoln, and war.

Harriet felt badgered in her Civics class. Her professor was growing angrier every day. One day he yelled at the girls and said "you girls don't even know a Negro, do you?" Harriet made the mistake of raising her hand and said, "yes, I do, our servant, Sassy, is a Negro." The room went silent. "Your servant, or your slave?" he asked. Harriet insisted Sassy was not a slave and that Sassy loved her and took good care of her. The professor asked questions like, where does she live? is her home as nice as yours? does she go to your church? does she sit at your table and eat with you? does she have a last name? does she have a husband? does she go to school and learn to read and write? does she own property? can she get a job at the post? can her husband vote? And on and on he went until Harriet realized, sadly, that Sassy was indeed a second class citizen in her very own loving home in Millersburg, Ohio. Harriet now had to rethink if she was merely an anti-slavery proponent or a red blooded abolitionist. She didn't know. She could see both sides. Her father was anti-slavery but believed in states' rights and did not want to fight a war over slavery. Billy was willing to go to war and die to end slavery for good everywhere. Harriet was on the fence.

Her education had provided her the knowledge to understand both sides and the empathy to accept both sides and the wisdom to know when and where to speak her mind.

CHAPTER 7

HOMECOMING

———— ❦ ————

1860

HARRIET COULD NOT WAIT TO get home to Millersburg. She was eager to see her brother John Fletcher and their new baby girl Florence. When John Fletcher had returned to Ohio from California he had followed his father's advice. He found a wife. Her name was Sarah but everyone called her Sally. He found and purchased land in Illinois. He settled in Florence, Stephenson County. She could not wait to hear more about John Fletcher's new homestead in Illinois. She could not wait to hear about his work on the Lincoln campaign. She could not wait to hear about his own campaign to become a member of the Illinois Legislature. She was increasingly her oldest brother's biggest admirer, especially after she learned of his role to secure women's property rights out in California. She looked forward to open conversations with John Fletcher about horticulture practices and agriculture prices, slavery and war, California and Hawaii. These were conversations she knew she would not be having with her own father, Joseph. With Joseph, it was always his way alone. However, Harriet did feel her father was on the side of right ... most of the time.

Harriet also was eager to see her brother Rollin and her beloved sister-in-law Sarah and their new baby. Harriet Louise was disappointed that Rollin and Sarah had moved so far away to Illinois which meant she would not see Sarah very often like before. [53]

Harriet's homecoming in June of 1860 could not have been more wonderful. John Fletcher and Rollin Valentine and their families were all back in Millersburg. John Fletcher and Rollin and their families traveled from

Illinois back to Millersburg to have a family reunion. Even the large home of Joseph and Harriet Susanna could not hold everyone now, so Rollin's and John's families stayed in the Hotel Millersburg. The town was a buzz watching the return of the successful brothers and their well equipped carriages, fine horses, beautiful wives and families. John Fletcher was interviewed by the Millersburg newspaper editor about California. He wrote an article about John's past role in the first California Legislature and his current campaign for Legislator in the Illinois State House of Representatives. [54]

The real talk of the town though was the brother who was not home, Peter Dewalt. He could not be at the homecoming. He was out in the wild, wild west and mining for gold in a place called Gold Hill Settlement. Peter married Ellen while in Iowa and they took off together to the Gold Hill Settlement. [55] Father was not one hundred percent in favor of this exploration, and yet he was somewhat in favor of it because the expected payoff was quite lucrative. Peter was the subject of talk around the table and everyone wondered what life was like out west with no laws, abolition skirmishes, Indian uprisings and no doctors and lawyers. Peter had fought in the Mexican War and was quite able to take care of himself and his new wife. Peter had found a wife in Ellen who was strong and resilient. Peter was not just a gold miner, he knew the land treaties and laws and about property rights. [56]

Henry wanted to return and be with the family when invited, but he could not leave his very large farm in Adams County, Iowa. Henry was very ambitious and worked tirelessly from sunrise to sunset. His much younger bride, he called Tina, was a good match for him. Henry was also the District Court Clerk as well as owning and developing farm land, so his responsibilities kept him away from the June 1860 family reunion in Ohio. [57]

Susan and her two little daughters, Mary Louise and Hattie, were constant fixtures at the Joseph and Harriet Susanna Ankeny home. They helped Harriet Susanna with all the preparations for Harriet Louise's homecoming. The little girls had taken over Harriet Louise's upstairs bedroom, and dolls and doll house, and many books and pictures. The granddaughters often slept in the bed that Harriet Louise and Mary Ellen shared for many years. Harriet Louise did not mind at all, not in the least. She adored the little girls and doted on them from the moment she got home. Susan promised Harriet that she would convince the little girls to come back to their own home so that Harriet could have her bedroom back. Harriet said the bed was big enough for three, for one grown up and two "littles". There was so much love and adoration among the Ankeny women and girls.

Mr. Barcroft, of course, came to all the dinners, but was enormously busy at his law practice. He was working closely with his Ankeny brothers-in-law concerning the many land deals they were involved with in Iowa and Illinois. He was also working with Mr. Josiah Given in his Millersburg law office. Mr. Given was a new lawyer who rented out the small space above the Ankeny's carriage house. Mr. Barcroft and Mr. Given were becoming well known as the best lawyers in the country, maybe only second to the highly esteemed Mr. Abraham Lincoln. [58]

Mary Ellen was not home when Harriet returned to Ohio. She would be on her way home as soon as the school where she was teaching was released for the summer. She had moved out of the house and was living on her own and courting a distinguished business man named Henry Clark. Harriet Louise of course wanted to see Mary Ellen but did not look forward to the reunion with her as much as she did with her adventuresome older brothers. Stories of the wild west and innovative farming practices and running for political office were much more interesting to her than hearing about Mary Ellen's school teaching stories. Maybe Mary Ellen would bring her fiancé along which would be interesting, but then, again, maybe not. He was in the insurance business and Harriet Louise could not think of any business more boring.

And, of course, Billy. Harriet did not know what Billy was doing these days. Harriet could not get the thought of seeing Billy out of her mind. She did not get letters from Billy while away at the Hudson School for Girls Seminary in New York, and when she asked her parents about him, they never responded. She hoped he had indeed waited for her.

Seeing and being with her family filled Harriet Louisa's heart with over-flowing happiness. She loved homecomings and sharing stories.

First there were questions for Harriet. How was the train ride? How was the food? How was school? Do those Easterners really refuse to wear fur and leather? Then there were questions from Harriet Louise. Do you think Lincoln will be president? How does this new water closet work? How many bushels of apples did we harvest? And then, has anyone seen Billy Wiggins?

The first day and evening were filled with light hearted laughter and lots of food. Susan's servant, Louise, came over and helped Sassy with the food preparation and cleaning up the pans and dishes. Louise was from Germany and barely, if at all, spoke English. Sassy of course spoke English but could not read or write. Sassy did think she was the boss of Louise, and it was humorous to everyone but them, how they communicated with their facial expressions and hand waving and foot stomping. So much laughter and Harriet enjoyed it.

The second day, leftovers were eaten requiring less work in the cooking kitchen and more time for visiting. The men were in the parlor and talking politics, agriculture prices and investments in land, railroads and steam engines. The women talked about the grandchildren and how smart they were. They whispered about people in the town and in their church. They agreed that it would require more containers to preserve all of the fruits and vegetables that would be harvested this year. Harriet stood at the door way between the dining room table of women and the parlor room of men. She liked hearing about both. She enjoyed both. She did not want to give up one for the other. She wanted to be part of both worlds.

Then everyone insisted that Harriet Louise play the piano. They kidded her that she could play the piano but only if she promised to not sing. They all laughed. So Harriet Louise played and the family sang along. They sang their favorite hymns, they sang Pop Goes the Weasel and ended with Yankee Doodle Dandy. Then Harriet Louise played portions of a new tune, Autumn, which was part of a cantata that was written for the girls at the Hudson School to perform. The family stood on their feet and applauded when she finished. Life was so wonderful for Harriet Louise.

At the end of the evening the young families of Rollin and John Fletcher piled into the back of the open buckboard wagon. Harriet Louise and Joseph drove the team of horses and the families back to the Millersburg Hotel. They left their fine carriages and horses in the family's own carriage house and barn. It was there, at the hotel, that Harriet spotted him. There was Billy. As handsome as ever. He was working at the hotel. He was tending guests' horses, he was helping travelers with their luggage, he was cajoling a crying child with a stick of candy, and then he saw Harriet Louise staring at him. He hastily walked to her and almost hugged her, but then sheepishly, just grinned and said how happy he was to see her back in Millersburg. She grinned from ear to ear also and told him that they would see each other on Sunday afternoon after church. Harriet Louise did not believe in protocol when it came to dating or telling men what to do. She wanted to be with Billy and so she was not going to waste any time.

CHAPTER 8

HARRIET, WILL YOU WAIT FOR ME?

———— ⊗⊗⊗ ————

THE SUMMER OF 1860 FLEW by. Harriet Louise was busy with the orchards and gardens. She often watched Susan's little ones while Susan and her mother did volunteer work for the church or community. Harriet Louise worked in Mr. Barcroft's law office every chance she could. Harriet also got a paying job at the hotel working behind the desk, greeting visitors, handling their payments and taking money to the bank. Of course she was there for one reason really, Billy. Harriet and Billy learned to appreciate each other, their personalities, their smiles, their caring hearts. Billy and Harriet met every Sunday afternoon for a picnic, or a band concert in the park, or a church event. Billy declined Harriet's invitations to attend Ankeny family functions. Billy was reluctant to be around Joseph. He was intimidating. And, after all, Billy knew Joseph's skepticism of abolitionists and opposition to a war between the states. Billy heard Joseph's views often in the hotel lobby when the men of the town gathered to discuss politics and business. Harriet Louise and Billy too talked about the important subjects of slavery and the dreaded topic of war.

Mr. Lincoln won the election as President of the United States in November of 1860. But it was a hard fought race and a close election. John Fletcher Ankeny was active in helping Mr. Lincoln as well as running for his own elected position as Legislator in Illinois. [59]

Joseph was one of the electors who personally carried the vote from Ohio to Washington for Lincoln's election. When Joseph returned to Ohio he was worried. He was convinced from his conversation with Vice President Breckenridge that war was inevitable. [60]

Joseph disapproved mightily of slavery, but he was not an abolitionist, and did not want war. Joseph was historically of the Democrat party, but Joseph voted for John Fremont, who was the first person to run in the new Republican party as an anti-slavery candidate. Joseph then became a devoted Lincoln man.

The New York Tribune and editorials by Horace Greeley were frequently recounted by Joseph Ankeny. Ankeny was uncompromising in whatever he believed to be right. During the year before and during the great rebellion, there were frequent arguments and even fights in the town of Millersburg about the future of the United States. Joseph would join the local men for heated discussions in the smoke filled lobby of the Millersburg Hotel. Billy and Harriet enjoyed the conversation and took up the arguments themselves about right or wrong, slavery or states' rights, mass production manufacturing or craftsmanship. Harriet saw points from both sides. Her father was a fierce defender of states' rights even though he deplored slavery. Her Billy was a devoted abolitionist and was ready to wage war to eradicate it. Joseph comforted Harriet when she was alarmed over the strong feelings and language that divided people in her family, her town, and her country. Joseph said that eventually the feelings that run hot today will be softened and estrangements here today will be forgotten tomorrow and forgiven and friendships will be renewed and families brought back together. Harriet sure hoped so. Harriet was uncomfortable with conflict and harsh words. But Harriet did enjoy learning about and discussing politics and differing points of view about land management and eminent domain. She was quite capable of convincing and cajoling others to her way of thinking using facts and logic and proposing "what if" scenarios.

Just as Joseph had predicted, the states would erupt into a Civil War. Shortly after Lincoln's inauguration, southern states started proceedings to secede from the Union, fighting broke out in South Carolina and Virginia. On July 4th President Lincoln asked for patriots to enlist in the Union army. He wanted 500,000 volunteers. Billy wasted no time. He signed up and he was gone before Harriet Louise had time to fully comprehend what his departure would ultimately mean for her and their potential life together.

Joseph tried to enlist, but was denied, he was past the age limit for soldier duty. The Ankeny family was advocates of the Union cause and now stalwart advocates of the war policy and earnest champions of President Lincoln. Her brothers, Henry in Iowa and Rollin in Illinois, signed up. Harriet Louise wanted to sign up. However, the only role she could have would be to care for sick and wounded. Harriet early on knew that she did not want to be a nurse. She could not handle blood and vomit. She could not handle dirty diapers. So she took over Billy's job at the hotel. She cared for travelers' horses and carriages, she carried cases and trunks to patrons' rooms, she chopped wood, and did all the jobs that Billy had done in addition to her own duties of hotel desk clerk and guest room cleaning.

When Billy and Harriet kissed good bye, he asked, "Harriet, will you wait for me?" Harriet agreed.

CHAPTER 9

THE CIVIL WAR YEARS

⎯⎯ ✇ ⎯⎯

1861 – 1865

"we will live long to enjoy the society of our children"

DURING THE CIVIL WAR, JOSEPH and Harriet Susanna Ankeny were consumed with worry and talk about their sons and their daughters-in-law and their families. Harriet Susanna constantly bemoaned that wives and women had to do men's work.

Their sons, Henry Giese and Rollin Valentine were off to unknown and unsafe places. They were both heavily engaged in agriculture enterprises but they had wives with intellect and perseverance to keep the operations going during their absence. They had qualified farm laborers and servants to tend to the livestock and crops. Thankfully in Ohio and Iowa they were not worried about battles of war that were being fought in the south coming their way, for now anyway.

Their oldest son, John Fletcher, was an elected Representative in the Illinois Legislature. He commuted back and forth from the State House to his own house and farm in Florence and his wife, Sally, and his two young daughters, Florence and Mary Bird. John Fletcher was an ardent Lincoln supporter and worked tirelessly to support the Union in his elected role. [61]

Peter Dewalt tried to join the Union army but he was turned back. His previous Mexican war experiences had left him with some questionable afflictions. Peter and his bride, Ellen, had left Iowa and ventured out into the distant western territory beyond Iowa. He seemed to be removed from the actual prosecution and reality of the war. [62] [63] He wrote to his parents infrequently and when he did he just assured them that he was keeping up on all the legal requirements for acquiring land in Iowa and at the same time pursuing the very real possibility of striking gold in the western territory. He described the disputes in the western territory over the conflict about slavery. He was getting more and more involved with writing and speaking against slavery, and mentioned, briefly, about how abolitionists had come around and made trouble for the reasonable Lincoln supporters. Harriet Louise read her brother's letters and tried to "read between the lines" to understand what was happening in the unsettled west. She knew that some day she would have a great talk with Peter Dewalt Ankeny and his wife Ellen and learn some things about the wild west that letter writing could not describe. [64]

Rollin was quickly elected Captain out of Freeport, Illinois to manage the recruitment efforts. His intellect made supplies and clothing procurement and distribution efficient. He was quickly promoted to Brigade Quartermaster in recognition of his caring for the company. [65]

Henry joined Company H, part of the Fourth Iowa Infantry, and he also was quickly recognized for his leadership and made First Lieutenant. [66]

Henry left Tina and their baby daughter, Jessie, for war in July of 1861. Their hearts were especially heavy knowing that Tina would be giving birth to their second child in the fall and they had no way to know when or even if Henry would see his newborn child. Henry's first letter to Tina was written at Camp Kirkwood, Iowa. His letter was full of his daily activities and farm management directives for Tina. He ended his letter with "Kiss Jessie for Papa many times a day. Good night my dear wife." [67] Henry and Tina wrote letters frequently to each other. By late summer Henry was already on duty in Rolla, Missouri. Henry reported that regiments from Missouri, Kansas and Illinois were congregating but no uniforms were yet available. Henry was in charge of making out muster rolls and payroll, a duty he was well suited for after his experience as District Court Clerk in Adams County, Iowa and as the 1860 U.S. census recorder. [68] Henry wrote in September that his Regiment was ready to leave at any time for battles further south. He also wrote "it is a great pleasure to read your letters …. they almost make me homesick to see sick Jessie and you." Henry wrote and sent a letter about rumors of General McCulloch marching toward them, about eating peaches and apples, and their new Chaplain, without realizing that his beloved little Jessie had already died. Tina's sorrowful letter was received by Henry a week after Jessie's death. Tina wrote, "darling Henry …. may the Lord help you …. to bear the trouble that is our lot to endure. Our own little Jessie is taken from us. Her sufferings were short, but they are all ended. She died on the fifteenth …. She was more fit for heaven than earth …. How lonely this world will be to me without her. Can you come to me now? I am all alone….Oh Henry it is hard, very hard. We must endure it …. I cannot close my letter and yet I cannot write …. may the Lord help you bear this sad stroke. Yours forever, Tina." [69]

Henry Giese Ankeny
1827 - 1906

Henry's agony was overwhelming. Henry wrote, "My dear Tina, Oh how I love to write your name, it seems to give me strength and renews my overpowering love for you, and you alone. You do not know how dearly and how highly I prize your love, and your esteem. It is what I build my hope on, now and forever. What else can I expect to look to, for that love and affection, that buoy one's self above the throng that he is surrounded with. Oh Tina, without you this world would be a blank, a wilderness of woe and darkkness." Henry was deeply disturbed because he felt that he should be with Tina especially because she was soon to have another baby. Henry asked for a furlough and his feelings of grief were respected and he expected to get approval to return to Tina. Henry remained pragmatic in his letter and told Tina to have Jessie's grave fenced in and a stone cutter prepare a tombstone. [70] Then he added that the boys have their uniforms and will be paid tomorrow. The next day his practical decision-making dissolved and Henry wrote his deepest feelings, "My own poor dear Tina, This heavy bereavement that has stricken you down …. fell terribly upon me this morning. Oh God, I ask, why is this? But why do I ask? Thy will be done …. Our Jessie is gone from us, but I cannot realize it is so. No, she has only gone on before us and will guide us on to that land – the happy home where we shall rejoin her in her glory, to part no more, forever. This, my beloved, is our only consolation …. May God in his mercy bring that peace to us …. and cling to it for all time for thy sake, our own dear Jessie that now lives so angelically in heaven. Oh Tina, I know where I ought to have been in this great trial of yours, and would to God I had never left you to bear so heavy a load of grief and sorrow alone, but God knows I feel it to the very utmost of my soul. Oh, will you, can you, ever forgive me for this most flagrant wrong done to you and my dear Jessie, who is dead in heaven? What would I not given to have seen her once more in health, but even this has been denied me and we both suffer for my wrongs …. My head feels so heavy with pain, that I can scarcely see." [71] Henry declared that if he was not permitted a furlough he would resign and flee to Tina. He consoled Tina by reminding her that they would have another Jessie to love and cherish and encouraged her to be careful with her health for the sake of their unborn child.

Tina received a letter addressed to Henry in Iowa from Peter at the Gold Hill Settlement in the Western Nebraska-Kansas-Colorado Territory. The letter arrived a full two months after Peter had written it. Tina read the letter with great glee and wrote to Henry and passed on Peter's good news. Tina then forwarded the letter on to Joseph and Harriet Susanna in Ohio so they would know they were grandparents again. Peter wrote: "July 18 1861 From Our Cabin Having a little spare time from my paternal duties I take my pen in hand (that's an expression of the latest style) for to inform you of an event that took place on the 15th at about the witching hour of 11 o'clock in the morning after a few symptoms of the usual character in such cases made and provided by the fall of woman Ellen to bed and in an hour or so we were the high fallutin delighted high popaloouma hail Columbia Star Spangled Yankee Doodle Pap and Mam of one of the Ankeny. I tell you he is one of us – weights 9 lbs clean meat without his harness. Well he is a pretty fair specimen for a green one. Ellen is doing finely has been wanting to get up from the first day. Have hard work to keep her in bed hope to have her around soon. I hope so this thing of having a girl doing things less than half makes me mad done better before we get a girl. When are you coming to see us. Soon I hope. Anyhow when Ellen gets well. How long did Father stay with you. I have not heard from him since he left here. Things look bleak. Times is getting harder. What are we all to do. Ellen send her love so does the babby. Come soon as you can write sooner. Yours P D Ankeny" [72]

Sadly, by the time Tina read Peter's letter and she shared the message and letter with Peter's brother, Henry, and Peter's parents, Joseph and Harriet Susanna, the little high fallutin, yankee doodle Ankeny baby had died out in the forlorn Western Territory. Peter did not write a follow up letter to tell his family the sad news. Peter could not bear to write down the words.

Henry received a full month leave of absence for the additional purpose of recruiting for the Regiment for Colonel Dodge. Henry was at home in Iowa with Tina when their second child, Joseph Newcomb Ankeny, was born in October of 1861. [73]

Fortunately Rollin's assignment allowed him to return home to Sarah and his Illinois farm occasionally. And thankfully Rollin was home in December of 1861 when their little Joseph became ill. The blizzard prevented a doctor from coming to the home. Sarah and Rollin did all they could for the little two year old, but he succumbed to a terrible high fever. He died in their arms. They held a small service for the little one in Illinois, placed his life-less body in a wooden casket, and kept it in a frozen area away from animals until he could be buried in the Freeport City Cemetery. [74] They wrote to Joseph and Harriet Susanna about their terrible loss days afterwards. Why bother them, so far away, they could do nothing, too far to travel, middle of winter, war is going on. When the letter reached Joseph, Harriet Susanna and Harriet Louise in Millersburg, the women crumbled and Joseph said, "Now we have three little angels in heaven." Heaven held Rosina Bonnet, their daughter, and their two grandchildren, Jessie and now little Joseph. They did not even know about the little one lost to Peter and Ellen way out in the far away west at Gold Hill Camp.

Henry returned to his Regiment in Rolla, Missouri. He moved down the Mississippi River on a steamer and gun boat. Henry wrote to Tina frequently and to his father, Joseph, occasionally. His letters were full of interesting information, but always worrisome. He was involved in many battles, he saw men die, witnessed leadership incompetence, experienced frustration and longed to be home. [75] [76] Henry ended his letters with his favorite saying, "Kiss Josey For Me."

Henry's letter about the battle of Pea Ridge reached Tina in the spring of 1862. Tina read Henry's letter and held their son, little Joseph, tight. As always he ended with the words, "Kiss Josey For Me." Tina kissed little Joseph on the head, on the cheek, his hands, and over and over again and again and again.

When Joseph read Henry's letter about his son's proximity to the battles, Joseph immediately started lobbying his son to make contacts in Washington and with his state representatives to seek an officer position and station. Joseph recommended the change to Henry on the basis of increased compensation. However, Joseph really wanted the change to protect his beloved son, Henry Giese Ankeny, from harm.

Harriet Louise heard the news from the Millersburg telegraph operator. The words were few and bleak. "Orderly Sergeant Major William Wiggins of Ohio Volunteers died in Battle of Winchester, Virginia, May 23, 1862." Harriet felt numb. Somehow she had always sensed, felt, assumed, accepted that Billy's death in war was inevitable. The war had taken thousands of young men's lives. Harriet prayed to God for Billy's soul in heaven, then Harriet asked God, why, why, why. [77]

The body of William Wiggins was returned to Millersburg along with a box of his belongings. The coffin was delivered to the church. The box was delivered to the Millersburg Hotel front desk addressed to: next of kin, William Wiggins, Millersburg, Ohio. Harriet did not hesitate. She was not kin, she knew, but she was closer than kin. She opened the box. There were her letters to Billy. She didn't want to read them or keep them. There were some personal grooming items. There was his Civil War Cap. Harriet removed the cap, held it, caressed it, and then took it home with her. The cap was her only piece of Billy she would keep for the rest of her life. [78] There would be no more waiting.

On a cold, dreary and lifeless day, Billy was buried in the Oak Hill Cemetery; the same cemetery where Harriet Louise's sister was buried many years ago on a cold, dreary and lifeless day. [79]

Harriet Louise was sad about Billy, but there was no more waiting, she was planning a life ahead for herself. Her new life would begin and be in Iowa.

Harriet continued to work at the Millersburg Hotel for a couple of months while she planned her life. Her first life objective was to be with and support her sisters-in-law and their young families while their husbands were away serving their country in the war efforts and passing laws in the Illinois Legislature.

Harriet Louise traveled first to Florence, Illinois to see her sisters-in-law, Sarah, wife of Rollin Valentine and Sally, wife of John Fletcher.

Harriet was not eager but needed to see her beloved sister-in-law Sarah and somehow express how very sorry she was to learn about the death of little Joseph. She prayed to God to give her strength to comfort Sarah, and then she again asked God, why? Harriet wondered if Sarah had become sorrowful and sullen, like her own mother had, now that her child had died. She hoped not, because Sarah was what life was all about as far as Harriet was concerned.

Sarah and Sally both had little children and households and farms to manage. Harriet pitched in and helped with indoor chores of child care, cleaning, food preparation as well as the outdoor chores of wood chopping, animal feeding and gardening.

Although the three women were missing Rollin and John Fletcher in their homes, the three of them seemed to enjoy their time together immensely without the men. Their spirits were a little freer, more laughter, more silliness sometimes. They found that together they were quite able to run both the households and the farm lands and animals. They of course had able bodied male laborers to do the heavy lifting, but they were in charge, and it felt good.

Nevertheless, the happiest days were when Rollin and John Fletcher would ride back to their homes on their horses. The women and children would cheer and shout and feed the men and everyone was joyous.

Harriet always adored Sarah. Sarah taught Harriet about life. Now they were teaching each other about death. Sarah had lost a child. Harriet had lost the man she loved in war. They talked about their losses, they cried together. They decided they would not let death control their happiness like it had for Harriet Susanna for years. They would pray together to heal their broken hearts and ask God to give them strength and virtues to raise the next generation of Ankenys.

Harriet used her power of persuasion to convince Sarah and Sally, wives of the Ankeny brothers, that the future for the Ankeny family was in Iowa. She had heard so much about Iowa from her father. Harriet was heading to Iowa soon.

Then Harriet made her first journey to Iowa. Transportation was still not as easy into Iowa as around Ohio and out East. She hitched a ride with a group of travelers moving to Iowa in a covered wagon train. Her first destination was Fort Des Moines and then she secured a stage coach ride to Adams County. There Tina and little Joseph were waiting eagerly for her arrival. Harriet and Tina did not know each other very well yet. Horatia Fostina Newcomb – now Ankeny – was from the East and was born in Maine. They instantly became great conversationalists about the ways of the East Coast population. Harriet Louise was a tremendous welcomed relief for Tina for her spirit and for her physically. Although Tina had her own mother and step-father, Zachariah Lawrence to support her and responsible farm laborers to help her, Tina was near exhaustion taking care of a new baby and running a large farm operation while constantly worrying about her husband's safety.

Tina and Harriet bonded. Harriet had planned to return to Millersburg after a couple of months in Iowa, but Tina needed her help and Harriet loved living on the Iowa farm. Harriet Louise rationalized that her mother and father had their daughter, Susan and her husband, Mr. Barcroft, to help them in Millersburg. She thought now that Rollin had completed his military assignment as Division Quartermaster and Staff Officer to a General and had resigned his duties at the end of 1862, that Sarah and Rollin were stable and together in Illinois. John Fletcher made it back to his home in Illinois from the statehouse often enough that Harriet felt their lives and home were both stabilizing. So in the fall of 1862 Harriet decided to stay in Iowa and with Tina. They were busy preparing for the winter and waited impatiently for each letter from Henry Giese. He wrote often and was full of information about the war effort.

In the fall of 1862 from Helena, Arkansas, Henry wrote about his frustration with the war leadership accusing them of being traitors, plundering thieves, robbers and even murderers. He lamented that the great bane is speculation rather than patriotism. He expressed frustration with the defeats in Virginia but hopefulness that General McClellan was again at the head of the Army. He did not know what his future would be but stated he thought they would be heading to Vicksburg soon. Henry was elected Captain.

Henry also wrote about how much he missed Tina and Josey and rejoiced from afar that Josey was now walking. He wrote it is "a proud day .... our boy can walk. I think I hear you exult over the achievement, no doubt you are proud of him and it is a day to be remembered long years to come. But wouldn't I like to see him on his pins also carrying in chips, wood, water, etc. Yes my dear .... We will have an extra hand to assist us and we will do everything .... for a peaceful and happy home for us." [80]

Henry advised Tina to buy a stove to heat the home over winter. He sent money to Tina. He informed Tina that he had quit using tobacco. The winter days in Helena were somewhat dull for Henry, however, there was always looming danger. Tina told Henry of their son's abilities to climb high, higher and highest. Henry responded with the prediction that Joseph would be one of the greatest of the family. The lull was about to end for Henry. In November he wrote "I don't know what to write you unless to say that I love you and our Josey very much and think of you all of the time wondering when or if ever I am to see you again, for it certainly has been a century since we parted …. It may be a long, long time before we meet …. Tell Josey to kiss all that I love for me. Goodnight my dearest and my love. Forever your Henry." [81]

Tina secretly shared with Henry that Harriet was immensely helpful and welcomed but she was also quite bossy and demanding. Tina jokingly said that she wanted to replace Harriet with Henry. Henry wrote back and explained to Tina that his sister "Hattie" had been the youngest and badly spoiled and ruled the roost. "What "Hattie" wills must be the law with all that may come in contact with her or otherwise there must be a storm in the tea-kettle." Henry comforted Tina by asking her to "curb her temper suffi-ciently and pay no attention to her whatever, at least not when she is in anger, all will be smooth as a marriage." Henry understood Tina's plight living with "Hattie". He knew her well and described her as "passionate and loving by turns and being the pet has extensive sympathy with all." [82]

Harriet was indeed strong willed and at the same time compassionate. Harriet Louise and her brother Henry Giese were very much alike. They both were intelligent. They were excellent managers with good common sense and compassionate hearts as big as the sky and opinions even larger. But for now Harriet was Henry's replacement for Tina until the dreadful war ended and Henry was home again.

December in Iowa was cold and slow and dreary. Little Josey made Christmas bearable. Harriet's life was moving in slow motion. Henry's life, however, was a commotion. The last day of 1862 Henry was four miles from Vicksburg. Henry wrote the alarming words "we were in the slaughter pen yesterday" and he saw three men killed and eleven wounded and many taken prisoner. Later on a steamer ship Henry wrote "my time may yet come but I am in good spirits" and ended with "Kiss Josey For Me." [83]

After a brutal winter, spring finally neared. Henry and Tina, with Harriet's opinions of course, made plans for fixing the house, new plaster, making the flower garden, repair the fences for sure, and replacing the rag carpet. Differences of opinions prevailed, of course, about papering the rooms. Henry witnessed the most magnificent magnolia in full bloom in May in Mississippi. He also witnessed trampled planted fields after the army marched across. Henry received orders "to march" taking only what is on his back. "We leave in the morning for Dixie with twenty days rations." [84] Another disturbing letter arrived from Vicksburg in May of 1863 from Henry, "the artillery and musketry is in full blast. We have been fighting for four days. The enemy are now all inside their works. We have been on starving allowances for days .... Our regiment has a hill within three hundred yards of the enemy; perhaps we will have to charge them soon. Three thousand nine hundred prisoners taken yesterday. Can't say when Vicksburg will fall." [85]

Tina caught some kind of cold bug and then her lungs were congested and her fever rose. The doctor was called but it was Harriet's ceaseless care, along with time, that eventually cured Tina. Tina was worn down, ill, so sad to not have Henry by her side and yet so grateful for Harriet. Tina loved Harriet like her own sister or mother. In fact she loved her more. Tina really thought she would have died without Harriet. Tina did not write much about her illness to Henry, how could she, given the enormously dangerous conditions and worries Henry was enduring himself. But some day Henry would know the story of how Harriet saved Tina's life. Some day when they would all be together again.

By June it was warm in Iowa and hot in Vicksburg. Henry wrote that he thought they would have been in possession of Vicksburg by now. Henry reminded Tina, again, that if anything "should befall me while in the army, you must call on Rollin to settle our affairs and take care of you and Josey. I know of no one, unless Father, who could do better for you or him." [86] Tina's eyes filled with tears at the thought. Then she had another thought and she smiled slightly, realizing that she would not need Rollin or Joseph – she had Harriet.

There were rumors in Iowa that Vicksburg had fallen and the Union Army was in control of the city and fort. But it was Henry's letter dated July 4, 1863 that confirmed without a doubt to Tina that Vicksburg fighting was over and the rebels had surrendered. Tina thought this may mean a furlough for Henry, but not yet. Henry was ordered into Vicksburg after it fell and witnessed a filthy and devastated town with dead mules and horses and destroyed houses. Many men received furloughs but not Henry. Henry was contemplating resigning writing, "I am tired of this incessant turmoil." Then a furlough was approved. Henry and Tina were reunited in the fall of 1863. Tina had to share Henry with his many brothers and sisters and parents and nieces and nephews. The most glorious moments were seeing Henry and his son, Joseph -- little Josey, together. And then, Henry returned to war.

Henry believed there would be one more active and successful campaign to end the war in 1864 and to "teach the Southern chivalry that they must and can do without slavery." Henry was moving around and gave Tina explicit instructions to address her letters to "the 4th Iowa Infantry, 2nd Brigade, 1st Division, 15th Army Corps, via Cairo, Illinois." His letters were more positive and in November he explained that "sixty cavalry arrived from Nashville from General Grant for Sherman to report as soon as possible, at I think Huntsville. From there we will endeavor to flank Bragg, who we hear is falling back from Chattanooga …. We will flank him and force him to fall back. We have four divisions in our corps. Dodge is coming up with his division, so we will be able to go most anywhere or cope with a force that will most double ours." [87] Henry wrote that their campaign had ended and Generals Grant and Sherman were at his encampment.

Maybe Henry's attitude was more positive because he had just learned that Tina "was in the family way" and Henry implored her to "take the very best care of yourself, and in no case exert yourself too much, as you will require all your strength and fortitude to bear up this greatest of all wedded bliss …. and that we will live long to enjoy the society of our children." [88]

Harriet was feeling the war was maybe coming to an end. She envisioned the day she would return to Millersburg, Ohio now. As much as she loved Tina and her little nephew, Josey, she was missing her parents immensely. The work and the challenges of the Iowa farm were unique and interesting to her at first, but now, they were routine and less invigorating to her imagination. And there was no piano, few books and only Tina to have any serious discussions about life, politics, war, farming methods and religion.

Joseph wrote to Harriet Louise and told about his plans to sell the Millersburg businesses and their mansion and move to Iowa. He conveyed that Mr. Barcroft and Susan would soon be moving to Iowa to firm up land deals and establish residence there. Joseph assured Harriet that he had convinced John Fletcher and Sarah to move to Iowa also. Joseph encouraged Harriet to stay with Tina and help until Henry returned. Harriet understood Tina needed her more than ever now.

The war dragged on and on. The newspaper accounts of the carnage at Gettysburg made her ill to her stomach and weak in the knees. She imagined the cries of the men in pain. She envisioned the blood of the wounded. She could barely stand the thought of it. For the first time she had too much time on her hands and she began to think about how Billy had died. Did he suffer she wondered. Did he cry out her name she pondered. Finally, Harriet Louise, broke down, falling to the floor, sobbing about the loss of her beloved Billy and mourning the life they would never have. Then she began thinking about her brother, Henry, having to endure so much suffering, hardship and loneliness himself. Tina and little Josey then came to the forefront of her misery. Their faces and their needs pulled Harriet out of her self-pity, and up from the floor and upward and onward.

Harriet decided she would make time to grieve but it would not consume her. So she learned and practiced some new skills of embroidery, sewing, needlepoint, crocheting and knitting. She learned to use the treadle sewing machine. Instead of just helping Tina in the kitchen, Harriet took charge to bake bread, butcher chickens, can meat and create fancy pastries. Harriet would make the most of her time on the Iowa farm in Adams County, Iowa. Tina praised Harriet on her domestic accomplishments and told her she would make a good wife for a fine man some day. Harriet chose not to argue. Harriet knew her skills would be useful to her own parents as they grew older. They would need and rely on her when they moved to and lived in Iowa. She could not wait for the day when her whole family would be together and living in Iowa.

Harriet Susanna wrote to Harriet Louise and let her know the big news. She and Joseph had switched churches from the German Reformed to the Christ Church. No major reason was written, but she did say that the German Reformed did not welcome their servant Sassy and her family. So they all started going to Christ Church together. Without knowing all the details, and making some assumptions, Harriet Louise was happy about her mother's decision, and happy that her mother could make the decision. America was changing and the Ankeny family was changing.

The Christmas of 1863 was maybe the worst Christmas ever for Harriet. The war seemed to be going on in slow motion. Henry was still gone. Tina and Harriet sang Christmas songs to little Josey. Tina and Harriet did not bother exchanging gifts. Little Josey received one small toy of a wooden sculpted horse which he loved. The women told the story of how his father, Henry, road the horse into battle and saved the country from the scourge of slavery. It was Harriet who taught little Joseph his good night prayer: "Now I lay me down to sleep, I pray the Lord my soul to keep, If I should die before I wake, I pray the Lord my soul to take." She prayed that prayer every night with Josey but she really prayed it for herself.

The people of Iowa lost men and boys to the war but their lands were spared. Communities were growing, railroads were being built and enterprises were flourishing. Harriet knew there were good times ahead for the Ankeny family in Iowa.

The spring of 1864 brought news of renewed fighting and Union conquests, but the war continued on. Rollin Valentine was persuaded to return to duty to help in the war effort for another one hundred days. His incentive was he would be made a Colonel. Rollin was stationed in Memphis guarding the Memphis and Charleston Railroad. Henry was able to return to Tina and Josey on a furlough during the spring of 1864, but he went back to the fighting. In May Henry was elected Major of the Regiment but declined because he had no intention of staying in the military service and also because he did not want to leave the young men he had personally recruited from Adams County, Iowa. [89]

Henry learned of the birth of his daughter over two weeks after she was born. Tina gave birth to a tiny baby girl early in June. The child was not born on its expected date but the birth was fast and easy. Tina bounced back fast and the baby was content to sleep a lot and did not cry. Tina had become a leader in the community. She was head of the Soldiers Aid Society and active in her church. Tina managed her dependable farm laborers. Tina had many friends and her family near. Tina had become a strong, capable and independent Iowa pioneer farmer. Following the Ankeny family's penchant for fruit orchards, Tina planned and had planted one hundred apple trees, twenty-five other fruit trees reputed to do well in Iowa, and some grapes.

The best news was that Mr. Barcroft and Susan and their three children were now in Iowa. They loaded up their belongings and attached themselves to a group of travelers and came to Iowa in covered wagons. The Barcrofts had two covered wagons, two open wagons, nine horses and a one-horse carriage. They used farm laborers and Sassy's man, Mr. Gardener, to drive the horses and wagons to Iowa. Their destination was Oskaloosa, Iowa, where the railroad was being completed and where land deals were being sold and distributed left and right. The Ankeny family dynasty in Iowa was growing.

Soon after Tina's baby was born and settled in, Harriet wasted no time taking a coach to the village of Oskaloosa to see her sister Susan, Mr. Barcroft, her two nieces, Mary Louise and Hattie and her nephew Russell. Harriet Louise was interested, intrigued and excited about the new law office Mr. Barcroft established. Harriet yearned to work at his office again, writing out land contracts, personal wills, business agreements like she did long ago in Millersburg. But Mr. Barcroft did not request her help. Harriet asked Mr. Barcroft to help her get an education or establish work in the legal field. Mr. Barcroft would not help her. He reluctantly engaged in conversations with her about the war efforts, about the possibility of another Lincoln term in office, and the sad decline of the South's cities, plantations and industries.

Harriet contemplated whether to return to Millersburg, Ohio or to go back to the Adams County farm and be with Tina. She felt out of place in Susan's home. She was getting a lot of pressure to find her own man and make a life herself with him. Living with her sister and sisters-in-law was not a valued life circumstance in society. An unmarried twenty year old woman was encouraged to marry, and soon. With mixed feelings, Harriet returned to Millersburg, where she knew her parents would be happy to see her and she would be so very, very happy to see them. It had been a long time since she had been in Ohio. She knew she would be returning to Iowa some day.

Harriet Louise was welcomed back to Millersburg by her parents with open arms and tear filled eyes. Even her stoic father, Joseph, hugged her and became teary eyed at seeing her. She was so lucky to have such loving parents. It was a sober homecoming but a nice one. There were no parties, not until the war was completely over. Joseph was totally willing to talk about politics and the orchards and the prospects of starting a new orchard in Iowa with Harriet Louise. He had missed her. He explained where the land was already being surveyed and ready to purchase in Madison Township, in Polk County, north of Fort Des Moines.

In August of 1964 Henry was near Atlanta, Georgia. He was working on destroying the railroad and preparing to strike at Macon Road and fighting a great battle to get possession of the feeders of the Rebel Army. Henry had now been in the Union Army for three years. Tina's letters told the truth about their weak and afflicted baby, and Henry was writing about the dear little babe even at the time that little Rosa had already died. [90] When Henry finally got the news he declared he was resigning immediately and coming home and wrote "May God in his mercy spare us the one remaining joy of our past, present and future hope and expectations. While you, my dear deserted love, mourn for this loved one, remember that you have all my love and sympathy; that I, too, feel this loss, even so far and distant, but I hope soon to be with you again and never more to leave you. Kiss Josey for his Papa. Your own, Henry." [91]

As much as Harriet loved being back in Millersburg, Ohio she already felt Iowa tugging at her heart strings. She kept in touch with Susan. Harriet worried about the absence of letters from Tina. She hoped that her decision to return to Ohio had not upset Tina. It was Henry's letter to his parents that jolted Harriet with the awful news that little, tiny, sweet and quiet baby girl Rosa had died in August. Despair and emptiness filled Harriet. She wanted to be everywhere for everyone all the time. Transportation was too slow for her. She envisioned the day when her whole family would live in close proximity within the beautiful prairies and growing metropolises of Iowa.

Henry's promise to resign and come home was not fulfilled. His resignation was not accepted he told Tina. Henry continued to fight in Georgia. His letters about the battles now seemed matter of fact and his reports of deaths seemed like he was discussing livestock numbers or acres planted or jars of vegetables canned. One of his last letters ended with the now frequent checklist: hear cannonading five miles distant, we have to march soon, we will take this town, I will come home soon, write as soon as possible, kiss Josey for me. Tina was never so disheartened. Her hopes had been raised so many times and tragedy, despair and disappointment had taken hopes place. She was becoming numb and could not feel emotions of grief or happiness.

The fall election was heating up. Harriet went along with her father to vote on November 8, 1864. She went into the Masonic Lodge and watched her father and other men cast their votes. The last time she was even near this place her father had severely punished her. This time he allowed her inside, but only to stand on the sidelines and watch the men vote. Harriet Louise surveyed the situation, wondered why can't I vote, and then set in motion in her mind a series of actions that would make men realize that women should be allowed to vote.

Lincoln was re-elected in a landslide. The whole Ankeny family rejoiced. A series of monumental events began to cascade upon the country and upon the Ankeny family. Just when Tina could endure no more, Henry came home. He was mustered out on the 30th of November 1864. Savannah, Georgia fell to the Union, the U.S. Congress approved the 13th amendment outlawing slavery, President Lincoln was inaugurated again, Rollin Valentine was promoted to Brigadier General in a ceremony in Washington, D.C., and then, finally, the South surrendered. The telegraph in Millersburg was working overtime in 1865.

Harriet Louise delighted in reading her father's horticulture books and newspapers and political pamphlets. She visited the graves of Billy and the little sister she never knew. She impressed her mother with all the domestic skills she had learned while living with Tina. She continued to badger her father about moving to Iowa soon. She intended to set up a law office like Mr. Barcroft and told her father her plan and how she knew as much as Mr. Barcroft about land management and contracts and was an excellent writer. Harriet Louise told her father that she might also run for office as a City Councilman, or as a Legislator, like John Fletcher, when they move to Iowa. She said she would also manage the orchards her father planned to establish. Her father didn't argue with her.

And then from the pinnacle of happiness and hope, Harriet and her parents fell into the deep crevice of grief and despair. President Abraham Lincoln had been shot and killed. Harriet first saw her father cry when she returned home and those were tears of happiness. Now she saw him weep tears of sorrow. Joseph's admiration for Mr. Lincoln transcended mere admiration.

CHAPTER 10

ONWARD AND UPWARD – TO IOWA

———— ⊶⊷ ————

THE WAR WAS OFFICIALLY OVER. Life for the Ankeny families could have been easy and settled and even prosperous – living and doing what they had been doing. But Joseph had seen the promised land. His first trip to Iowa back in 1854 fueled the passion in him to make Iowa the future and forever home of the Ankeny tribe.

Rollin Valentine was a war hero. Illinois Governor Yates in his last annual message had paid tribute to the troops and recognized Rollin for his brave and honorable service. President Andrew Johnson and with the act of the Senate had brevetted the Brigadier General honor upon Rollin. [92] [93] Now Rollin Valentine needed time to escape the rigors of managing war efforts. He took the death of President Lincoln hard. Rollin had been one of the local men to welcome President Lincoln to Freeport back in 1858 when President Lincoln was there to debate Stephan A. Douglas on the slavery question. [94] Rollin Valentine was happy to be with his family and to tend the 320 acres of land near Freeport, Illinois.

Rollin was happy to be with his wife, Sarah and their three children but he was not necessarily content. He had strong ambitions and interests in land development, stock ownership in emerging corporations and the ever expanding railroads. Rollin and his father frequently discussed the role of the Ankeny family in Iowa and more importantly, Rollin's future leadership roles there, and to the country and to the public in general. Joseph envisioned Rollin as a very likely candidate for Senator from Iowa some day.

Joseph pleaded with Rollin to come with him, Harriet Susanna and Harriet Louise and move to Iowa soon. Rollin was interested but reluctant right now. He owed it to his wife and family to be with and nurture them in their Freeport, Illinois home.

Joseph, getting nowhere with Rollin, turned to John Fletcher. The two men agreed that Iowa was the place to be. Before moving to Iowa, John Fletcher had to complete his term as member of the Illinois legislature. Like Rollin, John Fletcher had great intellect. Both men had studied medicine which gave them the tools to think critically and be disciplined in problem solving. John Fletcher, though, was far more outgoing and genial. When Rollin was reserved and smiling, John Fletcher was talking and laughing. They both were devoted sons and wanted to please their father. Their father had put many demands on them both over the years and his power of persuasion was great. They both were also responsible husbands and fathers.

Peter Dewalt needed no coaxing about settling in Iowa. He and his father had established contacts and had pending land deals already in motion for years in and around the Fort Des Moines area. Peter's military service in the Mexican War seemed to change his personality. Joseph did not see Peter Dewalt with the same level-headed management attributes as Rollin or the exuberant self-motivation of John Fletcher. Peter tried to serve during the rebellion, but his mental and physical wounds from the Mexican War disqualified him from serving. So Peter did not feel comfortable living in Ohio where his parents lived or living in Illinois where his brothers lived. He did not want to be compared to his brothers' service and reputations during the war. Peter did not want to talk about his role in the Mexican War. The life Peter and Ellen lived in the untamed west and working at striking gold and managing shops, inns and services for the miners and their families was the right life for them at the time. When the war ended, Peter Dewalt and Ellen traveled back to Ohio. The family was surprised there was no child. Peter did not want to talk about losing their baby. He made many trips back and forth to Iowa to work on land deals which his law education prepared him for well. He carried information back and forth from Iowa and his brother-in-law, Mr. Barcroft, about land prices and deals and prospects. Peter personally selected and found the land in Iowa he wanted to homestead, near the post station of Berwick, in Polk County. Ellen and Peter Dewalt had not accumulated a huge household of furniture and did not own animals and equipment like John Fletcher and Rollin. Peter Dewalt was ready, willing and able to go to Iowa to start a new life.

Susan and Mr. Barcroft were in Iowa and already well established. [95] Originally they settled in Oskaloosa but when it was understood that Fort Des Moines was offering the most opportunities, Mr. Barcroft, being exceptionally astute, quickly moved the family to Des Moines. They owned land inside the city and built an exquisite home. They were already considered influential contributors to the city's rapidly expanding educational, utilities, transportation, medical and cultural affairs.

Mary Ellen was seldom seen. She wrote many letters to her parents. She told them of her home and life in Akron, Ohio, where her husband was a very successful businessman. It seemed as though Mary Ellen was not really one of the Ankenys. She was always distant and contemplative and sedentary. She did not have the spark and spirit of Harriet nor the fortitude and strength of Susan. But she found her own way on her own terms. She and her husband were perfect for each other. They were both careful and deliberate. They made their life decisions together, the two of them, without influence from her father and mother. Harriet sometimes envied that, to be that independent. But mostly Harriet wanted to be closely entwined with her parents. If she had to choose, she chose attachment.

In the year of preparation to the move to Iowa Harriet Louise was extremely attached to her parents in many ways. Her parents were getting older. Harriet helped them with some of their physical needs in the household and also in the orchards and with the animals. Harriet was of immeasurable help when it came to keeping records of finances, land contracts, crop yields and livestock records. Harriet Louise carefully kept family records of all the births and marriages and deaths. There were no divorces in their family. She wrote in the huge German Bible with leather covers with metal binding corners. [96] [97] [98] This was an heirloom from Pennsylvania and Harriet fully appreciated the family connection of the past to the current Ankenys and to all the Ankenys who would come after them into this world. Harriet's help was crucial to organizing and packing the household items. She carefully wrapped delicate glassware and souvenirs from travels, war, political and Masonic events. Harriet carefully wrapped Billy's soldier cap inside her doll clothes.

The large Joseph Ankeny family caravan leaving Millersburg, Ohio to go to Iowa was reminiscent of the impressive "best equipped outfit that ever left Somerset County Pennsylvania" to go to Ohio back in 1831. [99]

CHAPTER 11

IOWA – THE PROMISED LAND

—— ◦✸◦ ——

*"and let us all do our best to bring honor, dignity and prosperity
to not only the Ankeny family but to this beautiful and bountiful
land between two rivers that we now call home, Iowa"*

THE SEED HAD BEEN PLANTED in Joseph's head back in 1854 that Iowa was the place for the Ankeny family to put down roots, grow and prosper. Joseph had visited Iowa and selected land north of Fort Des Moines and he vowed to return and develop fruitful orchards and fine residences and prosperous businesses like he had done in Millersburg, Ohio. The Civil War and complexities of westward transportation delayed his dream. But now it was a reality. Joseph sold his properties in Ohio. Joseph's sons worried that this move was too much for Joseph "at his age". But, of course, when Joseph had decided something – it was going to happen. And Harriet Louise was right there along with her father supporting him every inch of the way. She was his best ally, convincing the wives of his sons that Iowa was the place to be. Harriet Susanna was the somewhat reluctant wife who found stability in her beautiful home and gardens in Millersburg. However, Harriet Susanna had also experienced a change in Millersburg. When they first arrived in Millersburg there was a bond among the people. Now she sensed boundaries. She even had changed churches. Society was changing and Harriet Susanna was open to change. More importantly, Harriet Susanna wanted no part of the narrow minded cliques who excluded the recently emancipated and newest citizens. So Harriet Susanna, too, was ready for a new life in a new land and shared the dream and embraced the vision of the whole Ankeny family being together in a land of abundance.

The Ankeny family was not the only family flocking to Iowa. The state of Iowa promoted land development and organized campaigns for settlers and investors, boasting the young frontier's rich farmlands, fine citizens, free and open society, and fair government. The proliferation of the railroads greatly facilitated the growth of Iowa and the Ankeny family.

Joseph relied heavily on Mr. Barcroft for legal and administrative services as they made their final move to Iowa. Joseph relied on Peter for finding and homesteading desired land in Iowa. And Joseph and Harriet Susanna relied heavily on their daughter Susan for domestic needs. Joseph, Harriet Susanna and Harriet Louise moved in and lived with Susan and her family in Des Moines while their own home, at the corner of Tenth and Locust streets, was being built. [100]

Mr. Barcroft was a well respected and successful lawyer in Des Moines. [101] Susan was becoming a well known wife of a prominent lawyer. Although Susan was not gregarious she always displayed the best manners, cordial atmosphere and exhibited the highest societal standards when the foremost citizens of Iowa gathered in their home. She managed four small children with strict discipline. They were to be seen but not heard. When Susan's parents arrived in Iowa and moved in with them, the children were happy. The two oldest daughters remembered well their fun times in Millersburg with their grandparents and their Aunt Harriet. The Barcroft children now enjoyed a few more pieces of candy, slumber parties on the floor of Aunt Harriet's boarding room and extended story telling. Aunt Harriet would read to them from books or their Grandfather Joseph who would recite stories from memory about the Ankeny family of Pennsylvania. Susan was a practical woman, so even though she disapproved of all the silliness, the attention paid to her children was welcomed because she could then attend to her priorities of serving her husband, homemaking, entertaining and community activism. Susan also was happy to have her family, who believed in the Lord, near her again. Mr. Barcroft refused to join a church. He was a solemn and serious man. He respected order, efficiency, diligence and competence. He also adhered to tradition and protocols and the structure of law. While in Millersburg, he eagerly allowed Harriet Louise to help him in his law practice because she was organized and a good writer. However, when Harriet Louise asked Mr. Barcroft to help her become a lawyer, he quickly discouraged her and encouraged her to find a husband. He was a man of the times. He was a prominent and foremost citizen of early Des Moines, Iowa and his dedication to important causes, the rights of man and universal justice were hallmarks of his life. [102]

Peter Dewalt was establishing his home and farm near Berwick in Polk County. He and Joseph secured more land. [103] They fenced the land and commenced to setting out an orchard. Joseph told John Fletcher his land was waiting for him. Come to Iowa. Soon. Now.

John Fletcher sold his properties and completed his responsibilities in Illinois and moved to Iowa in 1869. [104] John Fletcher wasted no time at all making his mark in Iowa. John's public service experiences in California and Illinois prepared him well to immediately become a leader in Des Moines and Polk County. [105] Even Joseph was no match for John Fletcher's exuberant ambitions. Joseph expected John to live on the land he had fenced and planted north of Des Moines. But John Fletcher never lived on the farmland, John Fletcher always lived within the city of Des Moines. John and his wife Sally and their four beautiful and high spirited girls were quickly accepted into the Des Moines high society. John Fletcher and Sally Ankeny were about as different from his sister Susan Ankeny and her husband John Russell Barcroft as night and day.

Harriet Louise often played the mediator among her brothers and her father. There was always some dispute going on. But it was always about tactics, property, timing or methods. It was never about family or politics or religion. They were becoming a family and business dynasty in Iowa. Many ideas were hatched, many alliances were formed, many decisions were made and many lives were forever formed and affected within the Ankeny family.

In 1871, Joseph and Harriet's new home was finally completed and they moved into the beautiful dwelling at the corner of Tenth and Locust Streets. [106] It immediately became, as did their Millersburg, Ohio home, the center of warm-hearted hospitality. Harriet Louise played a major role in the management of the new home. She organized frequent afternoon teas for the ladies and evening political meetings for the men. The home had all of the newest conveniences. It was decorated with a combination of heirloom and brand new stylish furniture. Harriet Louise made certain the bedroom for her parents was situated on the main level to avoid stairs for them. There was a beautiful staircase in the center of the home and a second utility staircase off the kitchen to the second and third floors. Harriet Louise's large bedroom was on the second floor with its own sitting area with fireplace. She had a closet the size of a small room that had a door to provide privacy and to hide the multitude of dresses, shoes, hats, parasols, fur stoles and coats, and jewelry. The servants' quarters were on the very top floor. It was one large room with movable partitions and four beds.

In 1872 John Fletcher was elected to the Des Moines City Council. John Fletcher became friends with Mr. Frederick Hubbell. Their friendship and business alliances gave John Fletcher access to land and railroad speculation insight. [107]

In 1873 Joseph and Harriet Susanna Ankeny celebrated fifty years of marriage on July 29th. [108] Their home was decorated with red, white and blue bunting on the outside. Fresh flower bouquets and all the best lace cloths and fine china and silver serving pieces adorned the inside of the house. Harriet Louise was, of course, the main organizer of the festivities. The celebration began mid morning with a long table full of baked delicacies and smoked meats and deviled eggs. Relatives and friends came and went throughout the day. Tea and a decorated cake were presented at 3:00 in the afternoon.

By evening many well wishers had passed through the doors and those remaining were the children and grandchildren of Joseph and Harriet Susanna. Their four sons and their wives were there with their many grandchildren. Susan and Mr. Barcroft were, of course, present and played a major role in coordinating the stationing of the many horses and carriages. Rollin had made the long trip from Illinois. Mary Ellen and her husband Henry Clark and their four children were not present. They did not move to Iowa from Ohio and in fact they moved even further away to Connecticut. Harriet Susanna felt incomplete because Mary Ellen was not present. Harriet Louise, on the other hand, did not really miss Mary Ellen. For Harriet Louise, even when Mary Ellen was present, she was not part of the Ankeny family's rambunctious get-togethers.

Dinner was served. Extra help had been commissioned. The children sat outside on blankets and ate finger sandwiches and cut up fruit. The teen-age daughters of many of John Fletcher's colleagues tended to the children, fed them, wiped their hands and mouths, and organized outdoor games for them. The adults sat at the dining room table at the corner of Tenth and Locust and enjoyed smoked turkey and beef, fresh string green beans and sweet corn on the cob from their gardens, fresh fruits from their orchards and more wedding cake.

Joseph and Harriet Susanna were the guests of honor but it was John Fletcher and his flamboyant stories of land and railroad speculation and propositions that had everyone's attention and imagination. [109] The show stopper of the evening was Harriet Louise when she dressed up in her mother's wedding gown of white silk trimmed with a lace ruff. [110] Joseph laughed and Harriet Susanna smiled. Joseph finally obtained the attention of his family and told the story of their marriage back in Somerset County, Pennsylvania. He pointed to the chairs and tables and some of the heirlooms that they still possessed and he encouraged his heirs to all treasure and honor the Ankeny family's past. He reminded them all of the heartaches and their many accomplishments. He encouraged them all to continue to be brave and free and love their families and their country. Then he added a new part to his already well-known paternal lecture. He added, "and let us all do our best to bring honor, dignity and prosperity to not only the Ankeny family but to this beautiful and bountiful land between two rivers that we now call home, Iowa."

While there was still a slight hush, Harriet Susanna spoke up. She spoke directly to her grandchildren. She looked out at her twenty-one grandchildren, ten boys and eleven girls. They were all dressed in fine clothes but the long day had led to untucked shirts, dirty knees, missing hair bows and damp, reddened cheeks from the heat. She said, "and to all of you little ones, you must know and remember how brave and courageous your parents have been during years of war and times of heartache. You are all loved very much. Obey your parents and study hard. Serve the Lord in all that you do. And when you need a shoulder to cry on" she paused and tried to look serious "go see your Auntie Hattie!" The adults busted out laughing and slapped their knees. It was so not like Harriet Susanna to tease and make jokes. The little ones were quiet. They soaked it in. They were the next generation of Ankenys. Then Irvine, the oldest grandchild, now twenty years old, spoke. He said, "We will Grandmother, we love you too." The loud laughter of the adults had turned to another quiet hush. It was a moment to savor. But the poignant moment was broken when the youngest grandchild at the party, little two year old Paul Lorah, let out a loud cry and opened his fist to release a bumble bee. Commotion ensued. Everyone had their own opinion on how to tend to the bee sting. Put ice on it, here's some lotion, rub it hard, don't rub it, do nothing – let him suffer – he'll learn, kiss it, don't kiss it. Paul's cousin, Joseph, who everyone still called Josie, comforted little Paul and said, "there there, don't cry, I'll kiss it for you."

When the sun went down, no one wanted to leave. The children were still in good spirits and collecting lightning bugs outside. Peter was sharing adventure stories about their exciting experiences out west at the Gold Camp Mine. Henry Giese was quietly listening and enjoying every minute. Rollin shared some confidential and eye popping tales about what President Ulysses S. Grant told him when he was out in Washington, D.C. [111] Rollin realized that night, then and there, that he was ready to move from Ohio to Iowa to be with the Ankeny family.

The 50th wedding anniversary celebration was a milestone not just for Joseph and Harriet Susanna but for the whole Ankeny family.

John Fletcher's pie-in-the-sky bragging about his railroad development turned out to be true. Frederick Hubbell and John Fletcher Ankeny became promoters and stockholders of a railway system from Des Moines to Ames. John Fletcher strategically bought an 80 acre tract of land north of Des Moines and south of Ames in 1874. A year later he platted the land and titled it Ankeny and secured the right-of-way rights for a rail line. [112] The name of Ankeny was officially given to the village in 1875. John Fletcher built a store and post office. He built a boarding room hotel. John Fletcher and Sally built a home on Walnut Street in the village of Ankeny, however, they did not move into that home, they continued to live in the city of Des Moines. [113] [114] [115]

Rollin's decision to move to Iowa was put into action. Rollin's astute understanding of how to supply and deliver goods and materials during the war prepared him to also understand that the growing towns of Iowa needed building supplies. Lumber was one of the growing industries in Iowa. Rollin went into the lumber business in Winterset in Madison County. [116] [117] [118] Their move went smoothly. Their daughter, Harriet Louise, met a young man named John Conger. They married in an elaborate ceremony and enjoyed a huge reception. Of course Aunt Harriet Louise who shared a special bond with little Harriet Louise was the host of the big event. John Conger was in the hardware business and so he and his new father-in-law Rollin became close business partners and involved with much of the construction of barns, homes and bridges in Madison County. Little Harriet Louise and Mr. Conger had a baby boy. He was named after his grandfather and the Civil War hero, General Rollin Valentine Ankeny. It was Rollin's first grandchild. It was the first great grandchild for Joseph and Harriet Susanna.

Rollin Valentine's reputed management skills were put to good use in Iowa. He was named the Treasurer for the Iowa exhibits and contributions to the upcoming Centennial Exhibition of 1876 in Philadelphia. [119] He was in charge of fund raising and enlisted Harriet Louise's help to host many teas and gatherings at the Ankeny home on Locust Street.

Joseph was visiting his son, Rollin, in May of 1876. His granddaughter, Harriet Louise Conger, and his first great grandson, Rollin V Conger, now one year old, stopped by to see him. Joseph was content. He was discussing plans for expanding Rollin's business. They were discussing the upcoming election of Harriet Louise's brother-in-law as Treasurer of Dallas County. [120] They contemplated how useful the very successful Mr. Edwin Hurd Conger would be to them in that capacity. Rollin and his son-in-law were eager to continue their foray into building the covers over the many timber bridges that crossed the many creeks in Madison County. They would like the inside help for securing the building contracts. The protected covered bridges were crucial to transporting agricultural produce to market and supplies to the many burgeoning commercial enterprises. Along with business Joseph and Rollin also reminisced privately and quietly about some of their most intense experiences during war. Rollin confided that the injuries he sustained at Shiloh just about did him in then and that they still continue to cause him discomfort and even pain on the most humid and rainy days. Joseph told his beloved son, the General, Rollin, "You are the rock of this family. John Fletcher is the lightning bolt that excites us, Peter is the sunshine that sustains us, Henry is like the great Mississippi River — formidable and essential, but you, Rollin, you are the strongest of all — the rock of our family."

Harriet Louise Conger brought out tea and birthday cake to her men — her father, her grandfather, her husband and her one year old birthday boy son. They were sitting outside, under an apple tree in full bloom, enjoying the warm spring afternoon. When Harriet returned to bring more tea, she saw them huddled together, Joseph collapsed on the ground. Harriet dropped the serving tray and rushed to her grandfather, her father, her husband and her son. Joseph Ankeny, born in Somerset County, Pennsylvania in 1802, died at his son's home in Madison County, Iowa in 1876.

Harriet Susanna and Harriet Louise were sitting at the dining room table eating their evening meal and complaining about Joseph's absence. They speculated that he had gone fishing and lost track of time because the walleyes were biting, or maybe he and Rollin are telling war stories again and they could not stop, or maybe they are just enjoying little Rollin trying to walk on this his first birthday. When Rollin Valentine entered the home without Joseph, the women stood up, without words they knew. Rollin wrapped his arms around Harriet Susanna and Harriet Louise.

The funeral was elaborate and long. It was sad but hopeful. What a great influence Joseph Ankeny had on city structures, politics, horticulture and culture. What a grand society of Ankenys he had created. [121] Joseph was laid to rest in the beautiful Woodland Cemetery. [122]

Mary Ellen and her family could not make it back to Iowa from Connecticut in time for the funeral and burial. [123] However, they sent their oldest child, Eunice Aurelia Clark, to represent them and Eunice arrived several days after the funeral. Harriet Susanna gushed and made over Eunice as though she were her only grandchild. Harriet Louise was not so enamored by Eunice but she made Eunice feel welcome and comfortable in Des Moines, Iowa. When it came time for Eunice to leave, she vowed to her grandmother and Auntie Hattie that she would return some day and make Des Moines her home too and the Ankeny family her family. [124] It was a sad good bye but a hopeful one.

Harriet Susanna spent hours crying and days just sitting and staring. Harriet Louise knew her mother in this condition before, back in Ohio. Harriet Louise also knew that it would be up to her to restore her mother. Harriet Louise kept busy. She wrote to all the Ankeny relatives, friends and business associates about the passing of Joseph. Harriet Louise read the letters to her mother to get her approval and then they both signed the letters and sent them.

Josephine Chorpenning – now Barron -- received Harriet's letter late in 1876. Josephine remembered well the days when Joseph had returned to Pennsylvania, after Josephine's grandmother, Framy Chorpenning, had died. She remembered with great fondness Harriet Louise. That was over twenty years ago. Josephine Chorpenning was now Josephine Barron, wife of David Barron. Harriet's letter to Josephine went to Pennsylvania first but found its way back to Iowa to Josephine. [125] [126] Josephine and David Barron were married in Somerset County, Pennsylvania and they had four scrappy little boys. They followed many friends and relatives who left Pennsylvania for a new promised land of rich soil and bountiful crops in Iowa. Josephine had so loved getting letters from Harriet Louise and she wished she could write but had not learned how. Josephine enlisted her oldest son to write the words that she wanted to convey to Harriet. She wrote: Dear Harriet Louise Ankeny, My deep sorrow for your father. He was a great man. You are a great woman. I remember our time together so well and always always always wanted to tell you how much. Now I will bring you up to date on my life. I live in Iowa now. Just like you. My dear husband and I traveled to Black Hawk County, Iowa just this year. We have four boys. They are only a hindrance and not a help on the farm. But some day they will help with the many farm chores. We live in a small but warm house. We have plenty of timber and water and food. We work from sunrise to sunset. But we are not hungry. We are Evangelical Lutherans and pray before every meal. A church is being built in Bennington. I will like having a place to worship and meet other ladies to talk about babies and lady things. My husband only talks about the low price of sorghum or how I should milk the cows better. I am a farm wife. I think you are a city wife or maybe you are not a wife at all. I beg you to write me again and tell me about your life and the city of Des Moines. Your girl cousin from a long time ago, Josephine.

When Harriet read Josephine's letter she immediately was resolved to go to Black Hawk County Iowa and see and talk with her cousin from the Pennsylvania tribe. Harriet was now used to the conveniences of life and servants and cleanliness and many food choices, but she was not afraid of, nor resistant to, being with people who did not enjoy her station in life. Harriet had compassion for less fortunate families. She made sure that food was delivered to the families passing through Des Moines to lands further west. Of course she had servants to prepare and deliver the food, but Harriet made sure it got done. Harriet was not adverse to getting her boots muddy or the bottoms of her skirts wet or even a blister or two on her hands. She dug in the gardens, pruned the fruit trees, filled in holes in the roads with dirt or rock, pulled weeds, and even strapped herself to the oxen yoke to plow the fertile black Iowa soil on Peter's farm. Harriet was thin and eloquent as well as strong and determined. So she would visit Josephine at her farm house and accept Josephine's way in life.

Harriet wrote back and told Josephine that she wanted to come and visit. Harriet explained that she could not get away until Mother was back on her feet again. Harriet was devoted to her mother. So much was happening in Des Moines. Harriet Louise handled much of the legal affairs now that Joseph was gone. She was totally competent to do so. Mr. Barcroft seemed to think he knew more, and he knew a tremendous amount about the law and social justice, but when it came to simple property rights and deeds and contracts and business transactions, Harriet Louise was the best. She was an excellent writer, organized, had good common sense and she could persuade convincingly using honey rather than vinegar tactics. Harriet started a stash of items to take to the Barron family in Black Hawk County. Hand me down clothes for the boys, a dress or two for Josephine, a shawl, a few pieces of china that she could live without. The mountain of gifts grew. The plan was for Harriet to travel to Black Hawk County during the summer of 1879.

Harriet Susanna was making progress and coming out of mourning. To lift her spirits her children had commissioned artist Jerome S. Uhl to paint her portrait. [127] This would require her attention for days to sit for that painting. Harriet Louise was busy every day and every minute. Little Harriet Louise told the family at Christmas time that she was again in the family way and she and Mr. Conger would be having a baby in midsummer.

In January of 1879, the unthinkable happened. The person Harriet Louise cherished and idolized and modeled her life after suffered an untimely death. Rollin's wife, Sarah, was visiting her daughter Harriet Louise, in Dexter, Iowa to help her with little unstoppable three year old Rollin. Harriet Louise was often ill and weak with her second pregnancy and Sarah had come to help her daughter. Sarah caught a dreadful cold that morphed quickly to pneumonia. Sarah died at her daughter's home.

Everyone was shocked and distraught, but none more than Harriet Louise. She had picked up and carried on after other deaths, including her father's, but not this time. Nothing mattered at all to Harriet Louise. Her precious sister-in-law Sarah, who had given her more time and affection and unconditional love than anyone, was gone. Beautiful Sarah who had named her own daughter after Harriet Louise, was gone. Like that, in a flash, too young, it was too much to bear. Sarah was gone. [128] [129]

Rollin was grief stricken as were his children. It was expected that Harriet Louise would be the one to manage the funeral, write the obituary, arrange for burial, even decide what perfect dress would adorn the beautiful Sarah in her casket. But Harriet Louise had dropped down to her knees and wept and sobbed until her head pounded ferociously. People were coming to the house, but Harriet Louise stayed upstairs in her bedroom. She was inconsolable. She was paralyzed with grief and despair.

So Harriet Susanna rose the occasion and assumed the role. Harriet Susanna was needed. Harriet Susanna helped her beloved son Rollin and his children say good bye to their beautiful wife and mother, Sarah Irvine Ankeny. A more dutiful wife and adoring mother did not exist. A more loved sister-in-law did not exist. Harriet Louise could not even attend the funeral and burial ceremony in Woodland Cemetery. [130]

A week after beautiful and young Sarah died an even younger George Russell died. Florence Ankeny and George Russell had only been married a few years and they had a little two year boy. [131] Florence was now a widow at only twenty-one years of age. As much as the Ankeny family felt sorrow for young Florence, they were consumed with grief, and it was the George Russell family who managed the funeral, took Florence and Fletcher into their home and gave them the support they needed. [132] Fletcher Ankeny Russell would grow up without a father. Little Fletcher was adored but mostly ignored by his grandfather, John Fletcher.

The Ankenys were in disarray and mostly because Harriet Louise was not doing her customary nurturing and herding of the Ankeny flock.

During January and February and March Harriet Louise visited Woodland Cemetery daily. [133] Her friends and family did not even recognize Harriet Louise. Her clothes did not match and were not pressed. Her boots were never clean. Her hair pins and brooches lay idle in her closet behind the door. Every day at the same time, Harriet steered the one horse buggy from her Locust Street home up toward Woodland Avenue and west to Woodland Cemetery. She stared vacantly at the ground where beautiful Sarah was covered. Harriet Louise was so unhappy, she felt tired of this life, nothing seemed important, everything was a burden for her. She pleaded with God to make it all a dream from which she would wake and Sarah would be there for her. She lashed out at God for the unfairness. She asked God, Why? Why Sarah? Why war? Why Sarah's little Josey? Why sickness and death? Why young Mr. Russell?

Harriet Louise barked at people when they tried to approach her. No one knew what to do. The only person who could have pulled her out of this deep crevice was Sarah, herself, and she was gone. One day, Sarah's daughter, Harriet Louise, paid her Auntie Harriet Louise a visit. To Harriet Louise, little Harriet looked just like her mother, Sarah. Somehow the vision of seeing Sarah in her daughter produced a spark within Harriet Louise's heart. Sarah was always there for Harriet Louise. Now Harriet Louise must always be there for her niece, her namesake, Harriet Louise Ankeny Conger. Slowly but surely they persevered together.

Harriet Louise canceled her visit to Black Hawk County that summer. She stayed by her niece's side as the younger Harriet Louise gave birth to her second child in July. Another boy was born in Dallas County, Iowa and they named him after his uncle on his father's side, Edwin Hurd Conger. Edwin Hurd Conger, the senior, was making a mark for himself in politics and was already a successful businessman. Harriet Louise fully supported naming the child after someone with influence and standing. It was the Ankeny way.

By fall things were getting back to order. Everyone had responsibilities to do. Harriet Louise had been through such a bad year and it occurred to her that if she did not travel to Black Hawk County soon, it would be winter and harder to travel. So she packed her bags and loaded the trunk full of clothes and items to give to the Barron family and took a two-horse carriage trip to see her beloved childhood friend and cousin, Josephine.

What would she look like she wondered. Would she even fit into the clothes she brought. And four boys, good grief, what a commotion they must cause. She brought plenty of books and toys and games for them. Her carriage driver was quite capable of finding his way out into the dusty roads of rural Black Hawk County. When she pulled into the farm yard in her beautiful new two-horse black carriage, the whole family rushed out to greet her. Josephine was stocky now, straight hair and no frills, her face looked tired and when she smiled many teeth were missing, but she looked like family to Harriet Louise. They hugged and swayed. Josephine admired Harriet Louise's dress and red cloak. The cloak was Tina's. It was given to Tina from Henry when he returned from war. Tina loaned it to Harriet for the cool fall trip to Black Hawk County, but really Tina wanted Harriet Louise to wear something other than black for a change.

Harriet Louise only saw three boys and the oldest boy was holding a baby girl. Josephine could read Harriet's mind and told her she would tell her all about the family later.

David Barron was stocky also. They did eat well. The boys were talkative and inquisitive. They asked about the horses. Harriet Louise felt so happy. She had not felt happy since January. Josephine was just what she needed. The two women were the bridges that connected the old families of Pennsylvania with the new families of Iowa. Harriet Louise was a master of conversation herself and asked Josephine about the cows and how to milk them, how to make butter, how to feed the cows. She asked about the boys' school. She praised the oldest boy, Irvin, with his fine reading skills and penmanship. She recognized the writing. It was Irvin who wrote the letters for his mother. Josephine explained how the boys go to the same building for school and church, just like the Ankeny and Chorpenning and Barron families did back in Somerset County, Pennsylvania, when Peter Ankeny and Nicholas Barron donated land and built combination school and church buildings for the settlers. [134]

Then David started talking and explained the newest methods of tilling the fertile ground and spacing and planting seeds and harvesting and storage. His knowledge of how to care for cows and pigs and chickens was astounding. He was proud of his milking herd. He was careful not to brag but he made it known that he was providing well for his family by selling milk to the town people. He talked about his animals with so much love it was like he was talking about his own children.

There was no guest room for Harriet Louise, so she slept on the floor in the living quarters but on a platform of many blankets and feathered pillows and quilts which made it as comfortable, if not more so, than her own fine bed and linens back in Des Moines. Her carriage driver had to sleep in the carriage, but he survived. He was also a Civil War Veteran and so sleeping in a carriage was not a hardship for him. He had indeed slept worse places. The next day Irvin and Simon got a special treat and were given a carriage ride to their school. David and Josephine had cows to milk and chores to do. The four year old, Joe, was in charge of the newest seven month old, Orpha. [135]

Harriet Louise laid out the gifts she had brought onto their table so the boys would see them when they returned from school. The gifts went over well. The dresses were a size or two too small for Josephine but she accepted them and said she knew how to alter them and would. Harriet only then realized that she had brought nothing at all to give to David Austin Barron. She recognized her oversight and said she was sorry for her negligence. David said no need to be sorry at all and he told her, "Your being here is the greatest gift to my wife and family and therefore to me." Harriet Louise was even happier now than she was yesterday.

Harriet did not know how long she would or should stay. The family was busy and worked all the time and harvesting was approaching. So by the fourth day she bid farewell and promised to return and invited them all to come and see her and the Ankeny family in Des Moines. Harriet Louise added and maybe the next time you will have three more girls to add to the four boys who came with you from Pennsylvania. Just like my father and mother did. Joseph and Harriet Susanna left Pennsylvania with four boys and then gave birth to four girls in Ohio. Josephine said, "Only God knows our future, but only we can make our future." Harriet Louise left Black Hawk County believing that the future was bright for the Ankeny and the Barron families.

The trunk was empty on the return back from Black Hawk County to Des Moines but Harriet Louise's heart was full. The fall weather was crisp and cool and invigorating. The leaves were turning bright crimson and gold along the Iowa River and many creek edges. Rather than sit back inside the carriage, Harriet Louise climbed up onto the driver's bench. There she could feel the fresh air, see the beautiful Iowa landscape and talk with the horse and carriage driver. Harriet appreciated the protection of the carriage interior, but she also relished the unrestrained freedom of the driver's bench.

Life in Des Moines was so much different than Black Hawk County. The Barron family lived a simpler life but required as much work and perseverance and a different kind of knowledge. The Ankeny families of Iowa were living in a fast paced world full of new railroads, new streets, new state and local regulations and laws. Mr. Barcroft was in the middle of many of the complex legal proceedings, John Fletcher was in the middle of the wheeling and dealing, and Harriet Louise was in the middle of local politics. Harriet presented a proposal to build a park and an orchard across the street from her home along with her neighbor Mr. C. H. Getchell. Mr. Getchell was on the Railway Board of Directors and his opinions and ideas carried considerable weight. [136] But when Harriet Louise presented the plan to the city, the project was rejected. Harriet Louise was accused of only wanting to enhance the value of her own property. Instead of arguing, she withdrew her donation of $500 to establish the park and orchard. Harriet Louise was practicing the art of walking away from a deal that did not suit her. She understood the best way to insult someone was to ignore them.

Rollin handed over his lumber business along with his two youngest children to his daughter Harriet Louise and son-in-law John Conger. Rollin Junior was a teen-ager and little Mary was only nine when their mother died. Rollin immersed himself in work. The indoor work and daily routines of managing a business and farm did not suit him. He chose more adventurous pursuits. He traveled to Florida, California and Oregon to survey land and draw maps. [137]

Rollin was widely praised for his ambition. Harriet Louise believed his ambition was a way to bury his heartache of losing Sarah. Rollin was appointed U.S. Marshall and returned to Iowa. He was quickly asked to serve in public administration roles of overseeing the County Farm which housed poor people and he served as the Polk County Coroner using his medical training. Despite war injuries, the tragic death of Sarah and a debilitating horse accident, Rollin was relentless in contributing to the growth, development and management of the city, county, states and country. [138]

Henry and Tina worked together as the best husband and wife team imaginable. They purchased a larger farm and lived in an enviable large home. After losing two little girls, and having six strapping boys, they were finally blessed with a daughter, Harriet Elizabeth. [139] All of the children did well in school, enjoyed community activities, excelled in music and other pursuits. But once again they had to bury a baby girl when late in life Tina gave birth to Ethel who only lived two months. Uncle Henry's advice was often sought by his brothers, nephews and towns people. He always displayed a quiet and determined temperament. His devotion to his family was unending. He showed respect and courtesy to all even when he disagreed with their politics or religion or demeanor. Henry was the one who Harriet Louise would talk with and write to about business affairs, personality conflicts, political wrangling or just plain old complaining. Henry was a listener.

Peter and Ellen raised a beautiful family as well on their farm near Berwick, Iowa. [140] Peter Dewalt Ankeny was dedicated to the land. He relished the spring planting and fall harvesting. He was an elected officer in the local Grange organization. He attended lectures given by the Veterinarians and Agronomists at Iowa State College in Ames, just north of where Peter lived. He also branched out and read and studied the newest scientific discoveries for growing fruit trees. His orchard was the envy of many. They also raised livestock but the land and its produce was Peter's love.

Peter studied and learned about the growing opportunities in Florida. He told John Fletcher about the huge potential for lucrative orchards and fruit farming. Peter was mostly just dreaming, but once that seed was planted in John Fletcher, he seized the moment and went to Florida and bought land.

CHAPTER 12

FLORIDA – THE PROMISED LAND

JOHN FLETCHER USED PETER'S RESEARCH and Rollin's land surveying skills and Mr. Barcroft's legal expertise and Henry's money to buy up a large tract of land in the citrus belt of Florida in Brevard County in 1882. [141] He was away from his family and his wife Sally a lot in the 1880's as he worked day and night to establish profitable citrus orchards and developed a pineapple plantation in Florida. Just as he had done in Ankeny, Iowa he also built the necessary infrastructure for a town and called the town Ankona Heights. He learned the value of hiring new immigrants for planting and fertilizing and pruning and harvesting. Henry and his financial investments were paying off in a big way.

John Fletcher Ankeny
1824-1886

There were many trips back and forth to and from Florida to Iowa for both John Fletcher and Sally. They maintained their home in Des Moines. Their widowed daughter Florence and her little boy Fletcher were a constant worry for John Fletcher and Sally. Mary Bird had married a very responsible businessman and they started and managed a dry goods store in the growing coal mining area of Centerville, Iowa. [142] Mary Bird told her father on Christmas of 1881 that he would be a grandfather again in the spring. Fletcher acted overjoyed, but he really could have cared less. His passion was his newly created empire in Florida and he could not wait to leave Iowa to get back to Florida. He demanded Sally and their two youngest daughters come with him and begin a life in Florida. Harriet was eighteen and Susan was fifteen and they wanted no part of this Florida move. They had many friends, including male suitors, and an active social life in Des Moines. They had become very close to their grandmother and Auntie Hattie while their parents spent so much time in Florida. But John Fletcher insisted and the family took up residence in Florida. Susan enrolled in school. Harriet began working in the family business as a bookkeeper and progressed quickly to the head of sales and distribution of Ankeny Fruits Company. Sally and her daughter Susan did not fit into the Florida scene and they convinced John Fletcher that they should return to Des Moines. Their home was waiting for them. Harriet Giese wanted to stay on with her father in Florida and work in the fruit growing business.

John Fletcher's ferocious appetite for adventure and extreme desire for success and recognition finally took its toll on his health. He suffered a heart attack in Florida and died in April of 1886.

His body was transported back to Iowa and accompanied north by his now business partner and third daughter, Harriet Giese Ankeny. There was of course a huge funeral. He was buried next to his father in Woodland Cemetery. [143] John Fletcher's mother was eighty-five years old and growing frail. However she was in fine health and physical stature and mentally as sharp as ever. So she mourned the death of her first born son but no more than she had mourned the death of her little daughter, Rosina Bonnet, back in Ohio when she was barely seven years old.

Harriet Susanna now was determined to find a way to bring the body of her little Rosina Bonnet from Ohio to Iowa to be interred in the Ankeny family burial plot in Woodland Cemetery in Iowa. [144] When her children tried to talk her out of this crazy idea, she responded, "If you can find a way to bring a grown man's body all the way from God-forsaken Florida, then there must be a way to bring a tiny little seven year old girl back to her family here in Iowa. It is where she belongs, with us."

Sally agreed to her daughter Harriet Giese returning to Florida and managing the business. John Fletcher and Sally had four daughters and no sons. Harriet Giese was the closest thing to a son they had and she displayed the confidence, temperament and determination of her father, John Fletcher.

Twenty-two year old Harriet Giese Ankeny replaced her father at the helm of Ankeny Fruit Company. Her days were full of business correspondence, conversations with bankers, supervising the workers, negotiating prices for equipment and promoting their products to Florida and the East Coast. In the evening she had no desire for male companionship, she was content with her busy life that her father had made for her in the fruit growing business. When she was finally emotionally able to sort through and clear out her father's personal items in his Florida bedroom, she discovered an unfinished quilt. Harriet Susanna had sewn the little squares of fabric together and sent the thin quilt top with John Fletcher to Florida. She thought that a heavy quilt would be too warm for Florida, and so he only needed the one fabric layer of carefully sewn together fabric pieces. Harriet Giese discovered the quilt top in John Fletcher's bedroom but not on his bed, but in a quilting hoop. Harriet imagined her lonely father, by himself, at night, quilting, by candle light. Perhaps it was how he slowed his ever imagining mind down to get to sleep. She imagined her father methodically stitch by stitch sewing the three layers together and sandwiching the wool interior batting between backing fabric and the pieced top. The particular quilt design was named "old maid's puzzle". Harriet contemplated that. How apropos. Maybe an omen. In the evening, Harriet finished the quilt using the needles, thread and quilt hoop she found on John Fletcher's Florida bedside table. [145]

Peter and Ellen and their five children visited the Florida orchards and Harriet Giese Ankeny late in the fall after harvest season and as a special present to Rose Bonnet who had just graduated from the State University of Iowa. [146] Peter felt a responsibility for the orchards and to the young woman manager, Harriet. He, after all, had put the crazy notion of a Florida orchard in John Fletcher's head. It was joyous for Harriet to have her uncle, aunt and five cousins with her in Florida. Rose Bonnet absolutely loved Florida. She loved the quaint house, or cabin as it was, that John Fletcher had built and where Harriet continued to reside. Rose Bonnet loved eating the fruits from the orchards, the ocean, the sandy beaches, the humid air, the warmth of the sun, everything. Harriet and Rose talked together late into the night about the pineapple plantation and the orchards and they talked about a boy Rose was in love with and intended to corral into marriage as soon as she could and Harriet laughed at that. Paul Lorah Ankeny was sixteen and made the best of living in the cramped cabin with his four high energy sisters, parents and his cousin. Paul was quiet and did not say so but he too was mesmerized by the new surroundings of Florida. On the long train rides back to Iowa from Florida, Paul and Rose conspired together to someday return to Florida and talk their cousin, Harriet, into letting them help her run the Ankeny Fruit Company. [147] [148] First things first though, Rose was eager to get home to her beau, Mr. Lewis, and secure him as her husband since he was a most promising newly graduated accountant and maybe the most coveted bachelor in Des Moines.

The next fall, after harvest was completed, Henry Giese Ankeny made his one and only trip to Florida. He and Harriet Giese wrote back and forth constantly about the business and Harriet relied on Henry's advice. So Henry was very involved with the Florida operation from a distance. Henry wanted a traveling companion for this long journey. Tina did not want to embark on such a journey and although she was healthy for the most part, she went in and out of bouts of weakness and illness. Their oldest son, Joseph, was married with several children. [149] John was just married in August. [150] "Harry" could have accompanied his father, but Henry found excuses for "Harry" to stay home with his mother. Rollin V was enrolled in college, and Ralph and

Harriet were in school. That left Warren to accompany his father to Florida. Warren should have been married by now, and he showed little interest in social affairs. He worked tirelessly on the farm. Tina said, "Take Warren he needs to expand his horizons." And so Henry and Warren showed up on Harriet's doorstep and she was again overjoyed to have family companionship. They shared conversations, meals, trips to the shore, walks through the orchards, warehouse inspections and stories about John Fletcher. Harriet heard about her father's adventures to California during the gold rush, about his prestigious elections to the California and Illinois state legislatures, she learned more of his prominent role in the founding of Ankeny, Iowa and influence on Des Moines politics. Harriet thought to herself, yes that makes sense, that is what my father was doing when I was growing up. He was always around, but never there. But Harriet did not feel sorry for herself or harbor any ill will against her ambitious father. She understood that everyone is different and has his own set of needs. She believed God made everyone unique. Harriet then shared with her uncle something that would surprise him. Harriet showed Uncle Henry the almost completed quilt. She told him that it was John Fletcher himself who hand stitched half of the quilt. Henry was silent. At first it was hard for Henry to even imagine John Fletcher sitting still long enough to do such a task, but his second thought was, well of course, we all need our moments of peace for inward reflection. A very rare tear fell from Henry's eye.

During this solemn evening, Harriet asked her uncle what he knew about the untimely deaths of her cousin Harriet Louise Conger and her son, Rollin V Conger out in California. [151] Henry said he did not know what happened and that his brother Rollin was virtually unapproachable these days. Henry accused Rollin of being excessively busy in order to keep his sanity after seeing so much war and losing his wife and then his son and now daughter and grandson so young within the past ten years. Henry added that he thought Rollin never was the same after his little two year old son, Josey, died in the cold of winter many, many years ago. Henry added, Tina and I lost two precious little daughters also while I was away during the war years. Henry was a quiet Christian. He and and his wife Tina prayed together out loud but he did not pray out loud with others. Henry took Harriet's hands in his and bowed his head, Harriet closed her eyes and lowered her head too. They sat together in silence and in knowing.

Then Warren noisily burst through the front door. His face was red and eyes wide. He looked frightened and angry at the same time. He told Harriet that her hired hands were evil rebels. Harriet corrected him and said, "They are farm laborers, not my hired hands, I do not own them, I pay them!" Warren shouted back, "Well they hate me because I am from the North! They called me names I won't repeat and I think you should educate them about the emancipation." He had Harriet's full attention. Warren then turned to his father and fumed, "and why in the world did you give me a girl's name – Bonnet?" Henry said, "Well that is a prestigious family name and there is no T sound at the end of that name, the T is silent, you pronounce it Bone Nay." Warren's response was, "Oh swell, I'm sure that will make a difference to that group of mongrels out there in the bunk house."

Harriet reacted with a typical Ankeny woman's response. Let's have something to eat.

As Henry and Warren were leaving Florida to return to Iowa, Harriet begged them to return soon and to bring Tina and others. Harriet especially implored him to talk to and convince Rollin V and Mary B to come to Florida. They had lost so much, their mother and then their sister and brother. And although their father was alive, Rollin was lost to them as well. Henry said he would encourage all and any of the Ankeny family to travel to Florida. He laughed that the Ankeny tribe was a traveling bunch. No moss grows under Ankeny feet. He then seriously advised Harriet that she may one day feel the need to return to Iowa, her real home. Silently Harriet thought, perhaps.

Until the day she returned to Iowa, Harriet Giese lived out the lives of the Iowa Ankeny clan and the events of Des Moines through the weekly letters she received from her Aunt Harriet Louise. It took Harriet twice as long as it should be necessary to read a letter from Aunt Harriet Louise. Her penmanship had grown crooked. Her sentences were disjointed. Harriet Louise knew perfectly well how to write in full sentences and paragraphs and with perfect grammar and immaculate spelling and beautiful penmanship, but she just got to the point quickly. Harriet kept Harriet informed over the years in her many weekly newsy letters. Examples of and excerpts from her many Iowa-to-Florida musings included:

To H From H: Mother – fine. Henry – angry with me – again. Rollin is Rollin. Fletcher Russell is spoiled brat. Stuffy Susan had party did not invite. YOUR cousin Eunice is living with Mother and me. YOUR cousin Eunice is getting married. Portrait of Mother beautiful. Mother is frail. Excursion to Oregon was monumental and mountainous -- train food satisfactory -- hygiene deplorable. Florida to Oregon is too far. Wish I could see you. I am coming to see you soon. Mother is strong. You must join D.A.R.. I am now on Woodland Cemetery Board of Directors -- I will get that place in shape. Flowers are pretty this summer. Drought claimed most of garden. New city water system in place, thanks to your Father! Dug a new privy. Lois left us in a huff, you know Mother -- new servant is Heidi she is cute. Harriet and James have another girl – named her Louise Ankeny – good name. Edith and Alice look like twins – Mary Louise dresses them alike – they are spoiled. Mary Louise and George went abroad -- Mother and I kept Edith and Alice. Mother is frail. Have your joined D.A.R. yet? Henry's children barely made it home before blizzard. Don't read the newspapers!!! Jack The Ripper will scare you, living all by yourself the way you do. Eager to see Washington Monument when I go to DC. Bought all the "littles" same present this year –box of Tiddledy-Winks. Glad Mother's portrait artist did not cut off HIS ear! I hope you join with Florida women to demand voting rights. Please read Susan B. Anthony because her position is clear. Peter says this new USDA will ruin farmers. Peter is Grange officer now. We must go to Paris – Eiffel Tower – you will need new clothes if we do. I remember Mother and Father going to World Fair in New York -- I was ten and had to stay home with Susan and Mary Ellen – that was a barrel of monkeys. Have you joined D.A.R. yet? Bankers and insurance men are taking over our city. I like to read Mr. Barcroft's new Wall Street newspaper front to back – you should too. Our City Council and State Legislature could use your Father – they can't make decisions. What do you think about electric lights? Edison killed that poor elephant you know. We are getting a telephonic device installed, Mother is worried about it but Mr. Barcroft insisted. Mr. Barcroft bought AT&T stock. I saw in Wall Street newspaper Mr. Edison lives in Florida, maybe he's your neighbor, pursue him, I believe a strong and intelligent man desires a strong and intelligent woman (I sound like Father). Our Capitol is exquisite -- we see it from our porch. We all went to New Year's party at Hoyt Sherman's house – he lives next to Woodland Cemetery – I wish I lived there. Too many people in Des Moines – horse droppings everywhere. Huge black smoke plumes are gushing out of the big Edison Light chimneys. We can see and smell them. [152] The poles and lines are being rebuilt in downtown. The hot light bulbs are okay but too bright. Mother and I use the kerosene lamps – just safer that way. You should see the new Continental Clothing House, just opened at Sixth and Walnut -- they tailored Mr. Barcroft's tuxedo for the governor's inauguration. I will send CCH catalog so you can have better outerwear and underwear. We ordered Roddewig-Schmidt crackers for Ladies Afternoon Tea - many compliments - Heidi carried all three large confection boxes home from Court Avenue. Did you like the new stationery? It came from Lathrop on Locust Street. Christmas gifts from Tone Brothers were a hit! Well the city progress people really did it now, our beautiful flower beds are destroyed – stupid sewer pipes. Poles and lines every which way here in Des Moines. You need to keep pushing your city for better services in Florida. Florence, Fletcher and I attended concert in park last night – mosquitoes bad. All male band playing all brass horns--it was free. Our new coal fired heater warms the house - so nice to feel warm in January – I don't believe in the good old days. Black Hawk County man elected governor – don't know him – I wonder if Josephine knows. Mother refuses to sit on the new indoor water closet says she will fall through the floor – you must persuade your Florida residents to build a sewer and water system. Are those slow-minded men still denying you seat at the board – tell them your Father built that town – someday women will vote and they will be sorry.

CHAPTER 13

GLORY DAYS AND FAMILY WAYS

—∞∞—

1880's and 1890's

HARRIET LOUISE WAS THE KEEPER of the family records and she could barely keep up with all the changes. Her nieces and nephews were getting married, left and right, and babies were being born almost monthly. Harriet had prided herself in always delivering a birthday letter and present and confection to her brothers and sisters, their spouses and their children on their birthdays. Now she also had great nieces and nephews to wish birthday greetings. She wrote every family change in the Ankeny Family Bible and she could tell you every child's birth date. She also kept track of her dear, shirt tail cousin, Josephine's family.

The Ankeny Bible looked something like this: [153]

Susie McCaughan, daughter of Harriet and James McCaughan, died in 1880.

Alice B. King, daughter of Mary Louise and George King, was born on August 7, 1881 in Des Moines, Iowa.

Ralph McCaughan, son of Harriet and James McCaughan, was born on August 26, 1881 in Des Moines.

Anna Elizabeth Barron, daughter of Josephine Chorpenning and David Austin Barron, was born on July 24, 1881 in Black Hawk County, Iowa.

Fannie Eve Barron, daughter of Josephine Chorpenning and David Austin Barron, was born on July 24, 1881 in Black Hawk County, Iowa.

Fannie Eve Barron, daughter of Josephine Chorpenning and David Austin Barron, died on November 18, 1881 in Black Hawk County, Iowa.

Ethel Ankeny, daughter of Henry and Tina Ankeny, was born on February 1, 1882 in Iowa.

Ethel Ankeny, daughter of Henry and Tina Ankeny, died on May 6, 1883 in Quincy, Iowa.

Mary Bird Ankeny, daughter of John Fletcher and Sally Ankeny, married Benson Ehret Israel on November 13, 1882 in Polk County.

Josey Ankeny, son of Henry and Tina Ankeny, married Elma Rogers on February 27, 1883 in Quincy, Iowa.

Jessie Valentine Ankeny, daughter of Joseph and Elma Ankeny, was born on December 27, 1883 in Iowa.

Julie Gurtrud Barron, daughter of Josephine Chorpenning and David Austin Barron, was born on April 7, 1884 in Black Hawk County, Iowa.

Blanche Ankeny, daughter of Joseph and Elma Ankeny, was born on August 31, 1885 in Iowa.

Daisy Ankeny, daughter of Peter and Ellen Ankeny, married Frank Owen Green on October 20, 1885 in Polk County.

Eunice Aurelia Clark, daughter of Mary Ellen and Henry Clark, married Webb Souers in 1886.

John Fletcher Ankeny, first born son of Joseph and Harriet Susanna Giese Ankeny, died on April 9, 1886 in Florida, buried in Woodland, Des Moines.

William Dwight Israel, son of Mary Bird and Benson Israel, was born on May 23, 1886 in Iowa.

Irvine Sample Ankeny, son of Rollin and Sarah Ankeny, died on September 30, 1886 in Des Moines, Iowa.

Ralph Dewalt Ankeny, son of Joseph and Elma Ankeny, was born on October 14, 1887 in Kansas.

Rollin Valentine Conger, son of Harriet Louise and John Conger, died December 17, 1887 in Fresno, California.

Henry Clark Souers, son of Eunice and Webb Souers was born on August 8, 1888 in Iowa.

Louise Ankeny McCaughan, daughter of Harriet and James McCaughan, was born in December 1888 in Iowa.

Rose Bonnet Ankeny, daughter of Peter and Ellen Ankeny, married Thomas Edgar Lewis on February 12, 1889 in Des Moines.

Harriet Louise Conger, daughter of Rollin and Sarah Ankeny, died July 20, 1889 in Fresno, California.

John Barcroft Ankeny, son of Henry and Tina Ankeny, married Louetta Devore on August 15, 1889 in Corning, Iowa.

Rollin Valentine Ankeny, son of Rollin V and Sarah Ankeny, married Elinor Randolph on February 27, 1890.

Fannie Clark, daughter of Mary Ellen and Henry Clark, married Charles Dexter Allen in 1890.

Chester Devore Ankeny was born to John Barcroft and Louetta Ankeny on April 10, 1891.

Irvine Randolph Ankeny was born to Rollin Valentine and Elinor Ankeny on June 26, 1891 in Seattle, Washington.

Helen Lucile Ankeny was born to Joseph N. and Elma Ankeny on October 22, 1891.

Marshall Ankeny Souers was born to Eunice and Webb Souers in 1891.

Sylvia Mary Allen was born to Fannie and Charles Allen in 1892 in Connecticut.

Mary Louise Ankeny, daughter of Peter and Ellen, married George Caleb Burnett on June 29, 1892.

Mary Bonnet Ankeny, daughter of Rollin V and Sarah Ankeny, married Frederick Heaton Hunger on December 25, 1892.

Susan Ankeny, daughter of John Fletcher and Sally, married Ernest Warren Brown on December 28, 1892.

Henry Horton Clark, husband of Mary Ellen, died February 15, 1893 in Connecticut.

Warren Bonnet Ankeny, son of Henry and Tina, married Osia Joslyn in 1893.

Elizabeth Lewis was born in 1893 in Florida to Rose Bonnet and Thomas Edgar Lewis.

Louise Pierson Allen was born in 1893 in Connecticut to Fannie and Charles Allen.

Russell Barcroft Ankeny was born in 1893 to John B and Louetta Ankeny.

Homer R Ankeny was born in 1894 to Joseph N. and Elma Ankeny.

Harry Ankeny, son of Henry and Tina, married Emma Chafee in 1894.

Leland Day Hunter was born in 1894 to Mary B and Fred Hunter.

Harriet Giese Ankeny (31), daughter of John Fletcher and Sally, married Delos W. Mott (63) in 1895.

Colin Clinton Ankeny was born in 1895 to Warren and Osia Ankeny.

John Sidney Clark, son of Henry and Mary Ellen Clark, married Florence Lane in 1896.

Emerson Ankeny Brown was born in 1896 to Susan and Ernest Brown.

Marian Allen was born to Fannie and Charles Allen in 1896 in Connecticut.

Harriet Louise Ankeny was born in 1896 to Joseph N and Elma Ankeny.

Edna A Lewis was born in 1896 in Illinois to Rose Bonnet and Thomas Edgar Lewis.

Florence Clark was born to Florence and John Sidney Clark in 1897 in Connecticut.

Philip Webster Souers was born to Eunice and Webb Souers January 6, 1897.

Louise Pierson Allen, 3 year old daughter of Frances Louise and Charles Allen, died on April 15, 1897 in Connecticut.

Mother. Harriet Susanna Giese Ankeny, wife of Joseph, mother of four sons and four daughters, died 1897, interred Woodland, 96 years old.

Florence Marie Ankeny was born in 1898 to Joseph N and Elma Ankeny.

Margarey Clark was born in 1898 in Connecticut to Florence and John Sidney Clark.

Josephine Chorpenning Barron, wife of David Austin Barron, mother of four sons and four daughters, granddaughter of Henry and Framy Chorpenning of Somerset, Pennsylvania, died on February 19, 1898 in Black Hawk County, Iowa.

Josephine Hunter was born in 1898 to Mary B and Fred Hunter.

Henry G "Harry" Ankeny Jr., 28 year old son of Henry and Tina, died on May 6, 1898 and buried in Walnut Grove Cemetery, Corning, Iowa.

David Austin Barron, husband of Josephine, died June 11, 1899 in Black Hawk County, Iowa.

Robert Ankeny Brown was born in 1899 to Susan and Ernest Brown.

CHAPTER 14

SCATTERED ANKENY SEEDS

———— ∞∞∞ ————

"this time it was not little girls with dolls and dreams
but women with children and achievements"

HARRIET LOUISE TRAVELED BY RAIL and coach from Des Moines to Ankona Heights in the spring of 1890. She found her niece, Harriet, looking like a fifty year old, which was twice her real age, and dressed like a man in trousers, boots and even suspenders. Harriet Louise brought new dresses and silky slips and under shirts and a reticule [154] full of her own jewelry. She kept the jewelry tucked in a secret pocket sewn onto her under slip, a trick she learned many years ago when she traveled to New York. Harriet Louise insisted Harriet keep the jewelry. When Harriet hesitated and claimed it was too generous, Harriet Louise responded with her new favorite expression, oh Bullfeathers! Harriet Louise thought and actually admitted, "When you wear those pearls you will not only be beautiful you will think of ME!"

Harriet Louise did leave an abundance of gifts and food and letters and memories with the people she touched during her life journey. She scattered Ankeny good will across the nation. The two Harriets affectionately referred to their now deceased brother and father, John Fletcher Ankeny, as "Johnny Ankenyseed" after the American folk hero Johnny Appleseed. The Ankeny family planted fruit tree orchards across America, from Clear Springs, Maryland to Somerset, Pennsylvania, to Millersburg, Ohio to Florence, Illinois and then Des Moines, Berwick, Ankeny, and Quincy,

Iowa — and now to where the two women sat in the modest house built by Johnny Ankenyseed in Brevard County, Florida.

Harriet Louise believed her advice and gifts to her nieces and nephews were welcomed, and even if not, she gave her opinions and mementoes out generously anyway. When a niece or nephew needed a pat on the back or deserved a "bravo!" she generously provided it. Harriet Louise believed that praising a child was an absolute necessity in raising a child. So Harriet Louise planted her seeds of care, love and appreciation within her nieces and nephews while her brothers planted their wheat, corn, pineapple, citrus trees and apple trees wherever the Ankeny families put down roots.

Harriet Louise did influence young Harriet Giese. The idea of returning to Iowa was planted in Harriet's heart and mind but she would never totally abandon the Ankeny orchards of Florida that her father created.

It was Easter morning in Iowa. Sunny and warm. Harriet Louise sat at the table and sipped her morning coffee and made a list of goods needed for their household. She waited for her mother before setting out the boiled eggs and Tones cinnamon bread. When her punctual mother did not come to the table, Harriet Louise had a dark and ominous thought. She stopped her writing, put down the pen and coffee cup, walked to her mother's bedroom and peeked in. Harriet Susanna was very quiet and very still. It seemed as though she was sleeping but she was sleeping in the Lord. She was dead at ninety six years of age.

The funeral for Harriet Susanna Giese Ankeny was organized and managed by Harriet Louise. She had anticipated and was prepared for this day, but still her heart was sad. She was her mother's devoted daughter. Inseparable. They shared so much together. They knew each other perfectly. A look, a glance, a sigh, a half-smile were all the two women needed to communicate with each other. It was up to the devoted daughter to carry on the family traditions and honor and reputation and stories. Harriet Louise was up to the responsibility. Joseph and Harriet Susanna Ankeny had prepared her well.

Due to the expected enormous number of mourners, the funeral was held in a newly built large church where they were not members. That was the first of many good and practical decisions made by Harriet Louise.

Woodland Cemetery awaited the "woman of natural culture and refinement who lived a life of good deeds and devotion while exhibiting the highest of morals and noble purposes." [155] [156]

After the pomp and circumstance of the elaborate funeral and burial, Harriet Louise was facing an empty home without her mother. Her nieces, Mary Bird and Rose Bonnet and Mary Bonnet, all stayed with Harriet Louise for a few days to help their beloved Auntie Hattie. The four of them reminisced about the time they all had a slumber party back in 1880 when Joseph had died and their mother and grandmother needed cheering and Mary Bonnet had just lost her own mother and was basically an orphan at ten years old. Back then Mary Bird had talked about college days and Rose Bonnet listened to the college stories and resolved to go to the State University of Iowa. And now, almost twenty years later, those girls were all grown up with successful husbands and little children. But on this occasion after the passing of Harriet Susanna, it was four, not five, women reminiscing about past Ankeny family get-togethers and games. They made fun of their cousins but in good fun. They especially gossiped about Fletcher Russell, twenty years old and the most handsome and eligible bachelor in Des Moines. They all agreed he was the spitting image of his grandfather, John Fletcher Ankeny and they also agreed that his wild and effervescent personality was the true blood of the adventurer John Fletcher Ankeny. The three young women talked of their own husbands' professions and successes, their homes and of course their own most well-behaved and smart children. Mary's husband was already a successful businessman and was in charge of one of the biggest coal mining and distribution businesses in Des Moines. Mary Bird's husband was a successful dry goods store proprietor in Centerville, Iowa. Rose's husband was a big wig banker in Chicago. Mary and Mary Bird discussed the coal industry and compared the quality and price of central Iowa coal with southern Iowa coal. Rose revealed that she and her husband had been discussing with Harriet Giese Ankeny the possibility of going into the fruit growing industry in Florida. They all laughingly agreed that they should all move to Florida. Some pretty big plans from the Ankeny women were being sewn that night. Harriet Louise was mostly quiet and just listened to her nieces' life stories. She had no husband or children to compare and contrast. She was totally content to witness and hear the stories from these three most amazing nieces. She was, however, now the matriarch of the Ankeny family and everyone knew it and took her seriously.

And so it was another successful Auntie Hattie slumber party at the Ankeny house. But this time it was not little girls with dolls and dreams but women with children and achievements.

Harriet Louise wished silently that her niece Harriet Giese Ankeny could also be with them. But she would see her niece soon. In her last letter from Florida she asked if she could come to Iowa and stay with Harriet Susanna and Harriet Louise. She made a joke about three Harriets under one roof. But now, there would not be three Harriets, only two. Mother was gone.

A beautiful tribute to Harriet S Giese Ankeny was published, "Mrs. Harriett Ankeney, widely known as Grandma Ankeney, died in Des Moines April 18, 1897, at the advanced age of ninety-six. Mrs. Ankeney came of German ancestry, her father being one of the pioneer preachers of the German reformed church in Berlin, Pennsylvania, where, in 1801, she was born. Here she spent the early years of her married life, removing later to Millersburg, Ohio, at a time when the trip was made by wagon. In 1867 she came with her husband to Iowa and has for the past thirty years been a resident of Des Moines and Polk County. Her strong, bright personality and the remarkable activity and vigor which she retained to the very last, made her life a powerful influence not only in her unusually large circle of relatives and friends but in the entire community." [157] Harriet Louise was not happy at all that the "other" Ankeney spelling had been incorrectly used. She would make sure that never happened again.

Harriet Louise had a new friend in her life and she was eager to introduce Mr. Mott, a recent widow and a suitor of Harriet Louise, to the Ankeny family. He came to Des Moines often and he and Harriet Louise would go to the finest new establishments and restaurants. The Savery was their favorite place. The food and service was impeccable and the furnishings and architecture the best in the city. One night, Mr. Mott convinced Harriet Louise to take a walk with him under the glow of the recently installed new downtown lights. Afterwards, Harriet Louise realized that it was actually safe to be near those new fangled lights. It crossed Harriet's mind that with mother gone, maybe having another person, like Mr. Mott, to share her days with would not be a bad idea. She also realized that a new century and a new way of life was awaiting her.

The letter from Josephine Barron asking permission to come visit Des Moines was the best news Harriet Louise could have received. Josephine wanted to show her respect for Harriet Susanna and to give comfort to Harriet Louise, just as they had done many years ago for her back in Somerset, Pennsylvania. Harriet Louise was eager to share the many wonderful sights, sounds and city lights with Josephine.

When Josephine arrived there was not much grieving or mourning and only a few tears. Family members were invited to the 920 Locust Street Ankeny home to meet Josephine. The first to arrive were Mary Bonnet and Fred Hunter and their little boy. They did not stay long, Mary was feeling uncomfortable and needed rest due to the pending birth of their second child. Harriet Louise drug Josephine to downtown shops and confectioners. They boarded the city rail and rode out to Woodland Cemetery. They walked the city blocks and went into the new Observation Building and Savery Block. Josephine was exhausted. After a whirlwind three day visit, they parted at the coach station and promised to keep in touch. Although they shed only a few mourning tears during the last few days, when they said goodbye both women cried and even sobbed their farewell, as if it would be their last.

A telegram was delivered to Harriet Louise. Telegrams were never good news. She remembered the busy telegraph office in Millersburg during the war. She was right. Harriet Louise could not believe the words she was seeing. Josephine dead, buried Mount Zion, no need to come, nothing you can do. D A Barron. [158]

The emotions swept through her. She wanted to go and be with Josephine, well not Josephine, but with her family, but she really barely knew them, David doesn't want me there, but I know Josephine wants me there, but, no, she's gone. Harriet Louise was unable to comprehend and accept this sudden and unexpected loss. They had just been together and they laughed and enjoyed each other so much. She had nobody, really, to turn to, who really understood her despair and their unique relationship and kinship.

Josephine was really the only other person who fully grasped the family history of Somerset County, Pennsylvania. There was that other Ankeney family who came from Pennsylvania through Ohio to Iowa. They were friends with Joseph but their exact connection to the Ankeny family was only whispered. It seems Joseph A Ankeney had a different spelling of his last name for a reason. Harriet Louise learned from her father in a whispered conversation she had, and promised not to repeat, that Joseph Ankeney was the grandson of Johan George Frederick. Johan was born after his father, Noah Frederick, had been killed by Indians in Maryland. Widower Dewalt Ankeny married widow Margaret Frederick. Dewalt Ankeny raised Johan Frederick as his own son and he then became John Ankeney. [159]

Harriet Louise was protective of the pure blood line of the family. When the Ankeney daughters sought Harriet Louise's help in becoming Daughters of the American Revolution, Harriet Louise was forced to either tell them the truth or navigate her way out by always being too busy or unavailable to assist. It was a messy relationship. Harriet Louise genuinely liked Rachel Ankeney who married Mr. Charles Getchell and wanted to be friends, but it was best to keep a friendly distance, so she did not have to spill the beans or spoil the family seeds.

Josephine and Harriet Louise were the only two who knew that ancient story about the Indian murder and how Margaret Becker Frederick watched with her two daughters the slaying of her husband and kidnapping of her two sons and then as a widow gave birth to a baby boy back in 1756 or was it 1758? Now only Harriet Louise knew this secret. Harriet deeply grieved the passing of Josephine, her conduit to the genesis of the Ankeny family from Pennsylvania.

It was some consolation to Harriet Louise when Mary Bonnet and Fred Hunter named their new baby girl, Josephine.

Harriet Giese Ankeny arrived from Florida just in time. She left the large Florida operation in the hands of qualified paid managers. She still owned and managed the Ankeny Fruit Company but she was feeling a personal pull to be with family. Harriet Louise and her niece Harriet Giese needed each other. They were so alike.

Mr. Mott arrived in Des Moines from Franklin County on another business trip. He was developing a supply line and negotiating the sale of his hogs to pork packing companies in Des Moines. He was staying at the Savery. [160] The two Harriets rushed to the Savery to have lunch with Mr. Mott. The three of them got along famously. They talked and talked and had so much to say to each other that they frequently were all talking at the same time and then laughed at that. By the end of the meal, Harriet Louise, a keen observer of human behavior and motives, noticed something. She could see that Mr. Mott and Harriet Giese Ankeny, only half his age, were engaging in more than casual talk. Their interest and knowledge of agriculture and markets and business acumen made them a perfect pair. Mr. Mott did not realize Harriet Giese Ankeny was so young. The Florida sun, hard work and neglect of her personal appearance made Harriet Giese look much older than she was.

Harriet Louise once thought that maybe the widower, Mr. Mott, might have potential for her. However, she did know there was no way on God's green earth that she would move to a hog farm. So, when the older Mr. Mott started to seriously court the younger Miss Harriet Giese Ankeny, Harriet Louise totally approved. Most of all, she wanted Harriet to be happy. Harriet was actually dressing like a lady now and that also made Harriet Louise happy.

Harriet Giese discussed the fruit growing business with her Uncle Peter Dewalt and his son, Paul Lorah. She saw potential in Paul to take over the Florida enterprise. Fletcher Russell was trying to weasel in, but Harriet sensed that Fletcher did not have the character traits or patience to work in a business that required daily routines from sunrise to sunset.

The two Harriets, Mr. Mott and as many Ankenys who could fit onto the front porch at 824 East Grand Avenue watched the majestic parade of horse and carriages driven down Grand Avenue from the Savery House to the site of the Iowa Historical Building. They waved at every carriage. They knew Mr. Barcroft was in one of them, riding with his colleague and now

Supreme Court Justice, Mr. Josiah Given. The newspapers reported that 10,000 people attended the festivities of the Cornerstone Placement. [161] The family walked down the street to hear the Governor and other dignitaries speak. Florence, who normally worked in the Records Department of the State Library, was enlisted to serve refreshments to the dignitaries under large canvas tent awnings. Harriet Louise enjoyed being so close to all the festivities and part of the action.

Some strange news from Black Hawk County arrived in 1899. David Austin Barron had hung himself in his barn. Harriet Louise was mortified. How could he do this to his wife, wait, Josephine was already gone. Harriet Louise still had not totally absorbed that Josephine could not be alive and walking the earth. They had just been together and full of life. But so it was. The message came from Anna Elizabeth Barron. Anna wrote the awful news and then said they no longer could keep the farm so she and her two sisters had taken jobs as live-in housekeepers and servants with Waterloo families. [162] Anna conveyed she enjoyed her family and liked her surroundings and the kitchen was a dream come true for her. She especially liked the supply of spices and baking good from Tones Company of Des Moines. Harriet Louise could not rest. She could not resist. She had a plan. She wrote to Anna and told her she was coming to see her and her sisters and she had a proposition but she wanted to talk to them about it in person.

Harriet Louise offered the three young Barron sisters to move to Des Moines and be her live-in housekeepers. She would pay them well. Harriet Louise just assumed they would. But they declined the offer, under some false pretense that they wanted to be near their home and brothers and nieces and nephews. Orpha Barron claimed she had a male suitor, Anna Barron insisted she loved her new family and their household, Julia Barron was just quiet and went along with whatever her older sisters said. Harriet Louise was not used to being told no. She did not understand the Barron family.

CHAPTER 15

HARRIET'S TURN -- TURN OF THE CENTURY

———— ⚬⚬⚬ ————

"it was great to be loved and protected but
also great to be respected and free"

HARRIET LOUISE WAS IN HER fifties when she had the epiphany that if she ever was going to change the world the time was now. Her health was good. She was an accomplished and fearless traveler since the time she took her trip from Ohio to New York when just a teen-ager, changing stage coaches and staying at strange hostels, along the way. She traveled by rail both east and west to Florida and to Oregon. She could even manage her own horse and carriage and make it to Henry's home in Adams County. There was no stopping Harriet Louise. She had plans to see the Eiffel tower but that was frivolous right now. Now she had to go to work on the Ankeny women and all the women of Iowa and secure their voting and property ownership rights.

Harriet Louise joined and attended the Daughters of the American Revolution Abigail Adams Chapter meetings regularly. [163] [164] She chaired many committees and service projects. She tried to believe in the Temperance League but only because they supported rights for women. Their fanatic religious edicts and liquor bans were not her causes. Plus her nightly sip of sherry made her ineligible for that organization.

The national D.A.R. put out a request for any and all able bodied and minded women to help with the collection, organization and storage of revolutionary war family genealogy records in Washington, D.C. at their

Harriet Louise Ankeny
1844-1921

beautiful historic building. This was it. It was her chance. She applied. Her past hotel and law clerk experiences, New York education and unmarried status made her a perfect fit for the position of Records Clerk. Harriet Louise enlisted the help of Mr. Barcroft's Attorney Office to sell the family home in Des Moines, she stored some furniture and household items at Susan's house, and gave many of the family heirlooms to nieces and nephews. Harriet Louise found and lived in a boarding house in D.C. on Massachusetts Avenue run by Minnie Marx. [165] Minnie was a musician and traveled back and forth to New York. Harriet Louise paid little attention to her landlady and the other boarders but was totally enamored by their uniqueness. The United States of America did indeed offer every opportunity and way of life for any and all people from all over the world.

Harriet Louise loved her work for D.A.R. She met many women and they had great conversations. She volunteered to work with and for politicians and government officials and local women suffrage groups to do whatever she could to get the information out that the United States needed a constitutional amendment to allow women the right to vote. Some states had passed such legislation or constitutional amendments, but it needed to be a right for all Americans. After all, black men could vote now, women should vote too.

Shortly after Harriet Louise was settled and fully functioning in her paid job, she received the telegram from Susan that Mr. Barcroft had died. Harriet Louise responded that she was not coming home there was nothing she could do. Mr. Barcroft had everything in order for his wife and children upon his death. Susan's daughter Harriet and her attorney husband Mr. McCaughan lived in Des Moines were well situated to take care of Susan's needs. There was really truly nothing Harriet Louise could do if she made the trip back to Iowa. She could pretend she was sad for Susan's sake. But Harriet Louise was not a pretender. She wondered if the other three children would return to Des Moines for their father's funeral. Harriet Louise had lost track of where they all lived. She thought Mary Louise and her husband Mr. King were maybe living in Des Moines but heard they traveled all over the country with his bridge construction work. They often left their two daughters, Edith and Alice, behind with Susan when they traveled. Susan never talked about their son Russell. Joseph was living in Atlanta, Georgia of all places. Mr. Barcroft was an accomplished citizen of Des Moines, Iowa, but like men of his days, he ruled the household and Susan obeyed.

Harriet Louise knew Mr. Barcroft when he was a young man and just starting his law practice back in Millersburg, Ohio. [166] It all started there. She remembered his intelligence and knowledge of the law and she recalled with great fondness the days when he let her help him with writing wills and contracts and deeds and organizing and filing documents in his office. He treated Harriet Louise well then. But when Harriet Louise came to him to help her become a lawyer herself or at least a paid law clerk, he scoffed at her and told her she was too old for childish dreams and to find a husband. Harriet didn't hold grudges but she did not forget either. Like so many of the men in her life, she admired and respected Mr. Barcroft, but she just wished they could see the world through her eyes. Women, including her sister Susan, should be taken more seriously. It was great to be loved and protected but also great to be respected and free. Mr. Barcroft was interred in Woodland, of course. [167] Harriet Louise told herself there was no need to leave her job at D.A.R. and return to Iowa, there was really nothing she could do. Harriet told herself that she would make it up to her sister Susan someday.

A beautiful tribute to John Russell Barcroft was published, "John Russell Barcroft was born in Cadiz, Ohio, May 13, 1824; he died in Des Moines, Iowa, January 20, 1901. He was admitted to the bar at the age of twenty-three in his native place. He first settled in Millersburg, Ohio, where he engaged in the practice of law. While residing there he was for a time a law partner of Gen. Josiah Given, Chief Justice of Iowa. He came to Iowa in 1864, stopping awhile in Oskaloosa, but settled in Des Moines in 1865, where he entered into a law partnership with J. S. Polk and F. M. Hubbell. He was a man of much ability and occupied a commanding position in his profession, but had never been an office-holder, nor was he a member of any church or of any secret order." [168]

Susan wrote Harriet a nice long letter and fully described the prestigious funeral for Mr. Barcroft. Susan said she understood why Harriet did not return to Des Moines and even reassured Harriet that she had made the right decision. Susan then added that she would be selling their big home on 1717 Tenth Street and was moving closer to Woodland Cemetery and said she had her eye on a new type of small bungalow home that would be easier for her to maintain. It was located on Ingersoll Avenue, a growing and well respected part of Des Moines. Susan reminded Harriet that they would have to make arrangements for moving, selling, donating or storing many of their parents' treasured items now stored at Susan's house. Susan suggested donating the items to the Iowa Historical Museum.

Later the same year Susan sent another telegram. General Rollin Valentine Ankeny had died. Harriet Louise telegraphed a response which said she was not coming home there was nothing she could do. Rollin was a remarkable man but it was his wife, Sarah, who Harriet Louise loved. When Sarah died and Rollin chose his extensive traveling expeditions over his own children, the relationship between Harriet Louise and Rollin shifted toward politeness only. She respected her brother immensely. His recent role as the Polk County Coroner and the Manager of the County Home for the Poor contributed greatly to the overall well being and progress of Des Moines and Polk County. [169] Harriet Louise believed, also though, that his family's well being was important and he was not there for them after Sarah's death. He was a product of his time in history. Harriet Louise did not fault him nor was she angry with him. She understood why he did what he did. Nevertheless, he was wrong. Family should come first. She also fully understood that when a man provides for his family with necessary comforts and financial security, it too is a demonstration of love. Harriet Louise always felt secure and provided for, and for that she thanked her father, Joseph Ankeny. Rollin was very much his father's son. Joseph told Rollin he was the "rock of the family" on Joseph's final day on earth. They were two of a kind. Two remarkable men. Two Generals.

Rollin Valentine Ankeny
1830-1901

General Rollin Valentine Ankeny lived a most remarkable life, full of accomplishments. [170] [171] [172] [173] [174] He was interred in Woodland along with a growing number of Ankenys. [175] A beautiful tribute to Rollin Valentine Ankeny was published. "Rollin V. Ankeny was born at Somerset, Pa, May 22, 1830; he died in Des Moines, Iowa, Dec. 24, 1901. He read medicine after his school days, but did not practice it as a profession. He settled on a farm near Freeport, Ill., where he resided several years. He entered the military service in 1861, becoming orderly sergeant, first lieutenant, and captain in the 15th Illinois Infantry. He was present at the battles of Fort Donelson and Shiloh. In 1864 he organized the 142d Illinois Infantry serving with it until the end of the war, when he was mustered out with the rank of Brigadier-General. He was connected with The Freeport Journal for some years, but removed to Des Moines in 1879, where he resided until his death. He had served in various public positions under the general and State governments, becoming especially well known locally from his discharge of the duties of coroner of Polk county for several years." [176]

Harriet Louise analyzed everything before acting. She was deliberate. She had values and positions. Some would say she was opinionated. Harriet Louise was a discerning joiner. She stayed away from the Women's Christian Temperance Union and the American Federation of Labor. Although they were proponents of women's suffrage, they had other agendas Harriet Louise did not support. She did like the message and methods of the National American Woman Suffrage Association formed by Elizabeth Cady Stanton. She wrote her brothers, and nieces' husbands and implored them to do what they could to persuade Iowa to accept women's suffrage. Her messages fell on deaf ears and blind eyes. They were convinced that women already had fair and good treatment. They believed the protectionist laws helped women so they would not have to bear the stress and anxiety of men. The men's hearts were in the right place, but they were wrong. They were a product of their time in history. Harriet Louise did not fault them nor was she angry with them. She understood why they thought the way they did. Nevertheless, they were wrong. Empathy was Harriet's strong suit. She could understand and accept differing opinions but did not have to agree with them.

Florence wrote to and informed Harriet Louise of her mother's death two weeks after Sally's funeral. Florence purposely postponed the message so that Harriet Louise would not feel guilty about not being in Des Moines for the funeral. Harriet Louise's memories of her and Sally and Sarah together on the Illinois farms during the Civil War came flooding back. Now Sally and Sarah were with the Lord and with their husbands and buried in the beautiful Woodland Cemetery. [177]

After several years living in Washington, D.C. and having no Iowa family visitors, Harriet Louise yearned to return to Iowa. She received an invitation to a wedding party for Anna Elizabeth Barron, daughter of her shirt tail cousin Josephine, in Black Hawk County. [178] Anna included a short letter and said she was doing well and was marrying a most interesting chap from Illinois, John Henry Rigdon. John had come to Iowa with his brother, George, and he was very smart, articulate, promising farmer and was a winner of numerous debate competitions. Anna ended her letter with the benediction she learned from Harriet Louise. Onward and upward. Harriet Louise thought if only she lived in Iowa she would attend that wedding party and meet this interesting man. He might have possibilities for political influence. She sent a nice note on her best stationery wishing Anna all the best. She would later send an appropriate gift by personal carrier when back in Iowa. Yes, she was going back. She made up her mind. She would need to find a new home there.

Harriet Louise maintained a cordial relationship with her sister, Susan, but she had lived with Susan twice before in her lifetime and there was no way she would do that again. Florence Russell and her son, Fletcher, were living on East Grand near the Iowa Capitol. [179] Florence invited Harriet Louise to move in with her. Florence was working as a paid staff Librarian at the Capitol. [180] She had worked her way up from a Paper Folder and one of the first women to work for the Iowa State Legislature. Her son, Fletcher, was, well, entertaining. Florence had just recently lost her mother, Sally. It was a good fit for Harriet Louise to move in with her niece. Florence had made it on her own after her husband died when Fletcher was only a toddler. She was a quiet, determined and respectful woman. Fletcher pretty much raised himself. It seemed Florence never disciplined Fletcher. The Ankeny women thought Florence spoiled Fletcher. Florence did the best she could without a husband. She loved Fletcher unconditionally and gave him all the room he wanted and maybe needed.

Fletcher was entertaining and always conniving. He convinced his Uncle Ernest Brown to give him a job at Brown Distributors and Jobbers located at the prestigious 100 Court Avenue in downtown Des Moines. He flaunted his business cards and stationery and portended he was more important than he was. Fletcher wrote to his Great Uncle Henry Giese Ankeny and pleaded with him to support him financially and emotionally in his effort to go to Florida and make a name for himself in the fruit growing industry. He also expressed his desire to plant pineapples and become prosperous to his Uncle Brown and Aunt Sue. He cajoled them with the enticement that he would bring Sue and little Bob to Florida and teach little Bob to swim. [181]

Fletcher's experiences with the young women of Des Moines were legend. But none of them were pretty enough, cultured enough, educated enough or rich enough for him. Somehow he managed to meet Mr. Mott's wealthy niece, Grace Mott, from Franklin County. [182] Grace and Fletcher were married at her home in a magnificent celebration. Harriet Louise no longer was in charge of receptions and events. She attended the festivities and enjoyed every minute and appreciated all of the planning and physical labor as well as emotional labor that went into making such an event successful. Now, she wondered, could or would Fletcher actually make this marriage successful.

Four people were now living at 824 East Grand but not for long. Fletcher and Grace packed up and headed to Florida.

The Ankeny family was taking over Ankona, Florida. Paul Lorah Ankeny was mentored by Harriet Giese Ankeny to take over the Ankeny Fruit Company. Like Harriet Giese, Paul Lorah, was not married while he managed the huge and ever changing and risky fruit growing business. It took all of his attention. He insisted that his mother and father come live with him in warm Florida. Peter Dewalt and Ellen were too frail now to farm in Iowa. They enjoyed the change of scenery and climate and reminisced about the wild days they spent in the western territory in the gold mining district out in Colorado. They were adventurers at heart but totally practical in execution. Henry Giese Ankeny had invested money into the Florida operations and he wanted his own son, Rollin V., to keep an eye on things, and especially on Fletcher. Rollin V. and Edyth Ankeny became partners in the business. Rollin's leadership experience during the Spanish American War and his inherited intelligence made him a natural for managing the large citrus operations. [183] [184] He was also clever in new marketing schemes and used photographs of his own son, Harold, in advertisements for healthy eating and living.

Henry was making plans to travel to Florida. Tina, again, did not want to take the long train ride from Iowa to Florida, so Henry talked Harriet Louise into traveling with him. Harriet Louise needed little convincing, it was a great idea and they looked forward to the long ride to have long discussions about family, finances, father, Fletcher, the future. But before the spring trip Henry Giese Ankeny died on his farm in Corning, Adams County, Iowa with his dedicated, loyal and much loved, Tina, at his side. Their love for each other expressed even on their last day on earth as it was forever memorialized in their many written letters during their long absence from each other during the war. They endured so much together. Tina kept all the letters Henry wrote to her during the war. As she read through his love-filled letters, one message stood out to her. He wrote that he hoped they "will live long to enjoy the society of our children". [185] They did. They had raised a remarkable family. They had built a successful farming enterprise. They were pillars in their community and church. At Henry's funeral, the people of the town and his grandchildren were surprised when they heard the eulogy for this amazing man. They did not realize that this quiet, unassuming, man had been a California gold miner, that he fought in twenty-eight battles including Vicksburg and Pea Ridge, that he actually turned down a promotion to Major so that he could stay with and take care of the "boys" he recruited from Adams County, Iowa. [186] [187] [188] [189] Tina, his children, and his grandchildren were proud of Henry Giese Ankeny. Harriet Louise was proud to call him brother. His brotherhood of Masons added their customary end of life ceremony. A telegram from the National Military Parks Commission was read which expressed their appreciation for his dedication to locating Iowa troops on battlefields. His granddaughter, Jessie, who was studying to be a missionary, read from the Bible, said a prayer and reminded the mourners that Henry Geise Ankeny was now at home with the Lord. [190] At 78 years of age, Henry Giese Ankeny was laid to rest at the Walnut Grove Cemetery, near the land he loved, cared for, and called home for nearly fifty years. [191]

The work Harriet Louise performed at the D.A.R. national headquarters in Washington D.C. made her a valued member to the local Abigail Adams D.A.R. branch and a likely person to represent Iowa at the 1907 national D.A.R. convention in the District of Columbia. [192] [193] Harriet Louise packed her most beautiful gowns and jewelry and plenty of writing materials. She was very excited to be returning to Washington, D.C. She traveled with several other women from Iowa, Minnesota and Illinois. Their conversations were electric. Harriet Louise loved a good substantive conversation about government policies and laws, world affairs, finance and business practices. She enjoyed telling her own family history and hearing the family histories of the women as they all experienced the wonders of living in the freedom of the United States. Their main complaint was they could not vote, but they all had confidence that would change soon.

The national convention was as electrifying as her conversations with her new friends. She was among many delegates who visited the White House and met and shook the hands of President Theodore Roosevelt and his wife. She found time to do some serious shopping at her favorite store, Woodward and Lothrop of New York-Washington-Paris on their Friday bargain day. She found a satin lined mink scarf marked down from $10 to $2.50 and a Parame corset with real whale bone and elastics. She could not resist a new pair of Dongola kidskin button shoes with versatile Goodyear welt soles for only $2.50. In the Bri-A-Brac department she found many items to buy and return to Iowa and Florida including a new fangled two-piece grapefruit server, an inner bowl for fruit and an outer bowl for crushed ice. An avid writer like Harriet Louise was always in need of writing paper and she found the finest grades of writing paper and matching envelopes in D.C. Although she did not need any more dresses or suits, the latest style of Panama suit was so appealing she purchased the gorgeous gray with white broadcloth vest trimmed in velvet. It was no bargain at $38.00. [194] The Panama suit would be practical enough for traveling in a hot train and for trips to Florida. The Panama suit would also be stylish enough for her dream trip to Paris.

Harriet Louise wore her practical Panama suit the day she and Mary Bonnet Ankeny Hunter attended the large and widely reported Iowa Suffrage Parade in Boone, Iowa. Harriet Louise was very proud of the positions her niece, Mary Bonnet, held in the Polk County Woman Suffrage Society and the Political Equality Club. [195] [196] Mary's husband, Frederick Heaton Hunter, was the one, though, who was recognized with business and political talents. [197] Fred was elected to the Iowa General Assembly. Harriet Louise often counseled her niece that her outspoken opinions about suffrage, abolition and world peace could, maybe, possibly hurt her husband's ambitions. Harriet Louise believed that one wins more with honey than vinegar. But Mary Bonnet was her own person, well educated and articulate. Mary Bonnet lost her own mother, Sarah, when she was just a child. Her own father, Rollin Valentine, abandoned her after Sarah's death. She was raised by her older sister, Harriet Louise Ankeny Conger, and her Aunt Harriet. Her older brother and sister and her young nephew died early in their lives. Those immense hardships had honed her survival skills and perspectives on life and fairness. She grew into a fiercely independent woman.

And on this day in Boone, Iowa, these two women, aunt and niece, Harriet Louise Ankeny and Mary Bonnet Ankeny Hunter, marched together with thousands of women. They felt liberated and exhilarated at the power and purpose of all these women marching for the right to vote.

Harriet Louise was active in the suffrage movement but she continued to be careful not to be too vocal or militant. She had to maintain her friendships with many of the society ladies in town and they often thought whatever their husbands told them to think. Nevertheless, Harriet Louise enjoyed being a leader in the Women's Club and her persuasive way and energetic spirit paid off when they made her a delegate to the national Women's Club of America in Cincinnati. [198] Without responsibilities for maintaining a household she was now quite free to travel and socialize. Her Panama suit was perfect for that May trip in 1910.

There was no time to slow down for Harriet Louise. She was a veteran traveler and booked her trip abroad. The highlight was climbing to the top of the Eiffel tower on a warm, clear summer day. She was sixty seven years old and the most elderly person climbing. She paced herself, rested frequently, but she was not going to miss the view for anything. She had been dreaming about this day since the Eiffel Tower was built for the 1889 World's Fair. The Panama suit was one of her best investments. It washed up easily, dried quickly, and yielded to the hot pressing iron beautifully. When chilly she wore the suit jacket, when warm the suit jacket came off and the vest provided the proper modesty. The above the ankles skirt style was practical and Harriet Louise thought the only thing better would be an even shorter skirt or trousers, but that was out of the question. Fashion in Paris and London was exhilarating. Her ever-present parasol was at her side with her stylish reticule. [199] [200] Harriet Louise brought along only one hat knowing she would find one or more on her trip abroad to purchase. Harriet's hair was always tied up in a knot at the top of her head since she officially became a woman back in Ohio, and Billy noticed she actually had ears. After that, she never fussed with hair style. But now in Paris and London and seeing the exquisite hair bobs and waves, she considered making a drastic hair style change. She would thoroughly think that major change through though. She was more inclined to make a radical purchase like a motorized car before she would change her hair style. Europe was enthralling but not home. Although afternoon tea and biscuits in London were delightful, she preferred the pastries of the Des Moines confectioners. The London hotel modern indoor toilet seats with water reservoirs and pulling chains were certainly convenient, but she knew Florence's home was being retrofitted with a totally modern indoor plumbing system including a porcelain water closet while she was away. The milk, eggs and meat of Europe were nowhere near the quality of Iowa grown fresh produce. She recalled the last big shindig she threw at Peter's farm when she had persuaded the nephews to roast a pig from Mr. Mott's farm. Fruit was nowhere to be found. Maybe she should recommend to Fletcher that he begin a fruit growing business in France. Better not, he would try it. Dates and figs were not fresh fruit in her mind. The passenger ship was exquisite, and she met interesting people on the train, but she longed for her own quiet time and simple bed and side table at Florence's house, on Grand Avenue, in Des Moines, in the County of Polk, in her beloved state of Iowa.

Harriet Louise had begged Harriet Giese Ankeny – now Mott – to come with her to Paris. But Harriet Giese had declined the invitation. She was managing the large land holdings and farm operations in Franklin County with her elderly husband Delos Mott and insisted she could not get away. By the fall it was known the main reason she could not get away was because of poor Mr. Mott's declining health. The young Mrs. Mott was his full time nurse and caretaker. Mr. Delos W. Mott died late in November 1911. Harriet Giese Ankeny Mott was allowed to assume her husband's role as Trustee of the Agriculture College at Ames, Iowa until his term ended. [201]

CHAPTER 16

THE LAST CHAPTER

———— ⊱✦⊰ ————

"this IS family, we ARE the Ankenys"

"a regret is reserved for when a person does
not do the right thing and knows better"

SPRING OF 1912 FINALLY ARRIVED and Harriet Louise was ready to be more
active but only within Iowa, her major travel excursions were over. She
had seen the world. The reality was she did not have the energy to travel
extensively. She did thoroughly enjoy the daytime motor car rides around
Des Moines from her great nephew Robert Brown and his uncle. [202] She
now favored her own bed for her tired body. Every day she wrote to one of
her nieces, nephews and great nieces and nephews. She read the newspapers from front to back. She picked up some of her neglected needlework
projects. Her favorite pastime was visiting with anyone who was interesting
enough to listen to about the world, politics, new businesses in Des Moines
and flower gardening. She lamented about the state of affairs in the nation.
She attended lectures and programs but only when Florence would go with
her. The only meetings she prepared herself for were D.A.R. meetings. She
attended meetings of a rag tag group of young ladies who met at parks and
restaurants to scheme up ways to promote woman suffrage. She was the oldest of the group and sometimes she was not listened to or taken seriously by
the young women. That did not matter to Harriet Louise anymore. She was

learning from them and they kept her energized and intellectually alert. She had passed on her ideas and opinions to the younger generation her whole life. Now it was time for the younger generation to pass on their ideas to her. She passed on their ideas and flyers to her nieces and nephews.

It was almost a year since she had traveled across the ocean. When she heard about the sinking of the Titanic, she imagined what it would be like to drown at sea. The very idea that it could have been her in a sinking ship left her in a state of dismay for a week. Florence at one point scolded her obsessive and unnecessary worrying and said, "Auntie Hattie you must snap out of it!" Harriet Louise did snap out of it and decided for sure her traveling days were behind her.

When Harriet Louise saw the newspaper photograph of the suffragettes marching in a parade in New York City, she stared at the photo for the longest time. She longed to be there. She imagined herself there. She had traveled to New York City when she was a young teenager. She was an accomplished and fearless traveler. If only she could be a teenager again. But no, her traveling days were behind her.

Murders and suicides and war deaths were concepts that would sometimes grip Harriet Louise's thoughts. She read about a vicious murder in Villisca, Iowa when a family and their guests were chopped to death by a hatchet murderer. [203] Harriet Louise almost passed out when she read the article. She could not wait for Florence to return home from work to tell her about it and then make sure the locks on the doors were working and they actually used the door locks for a change.

Florence thought Harriet Louise was becoming a little eccentric.

The fall Presidential election became strangely crude and uncivil and dismayed Harriet Louise who understood the value of maintaining relationships and civility for the purpose of accomplishing her own objectives, always believing you catch more flies with honey than with vinegar. Because Harriet Louise had the honor of shaking President Theodore Roosevelt's hand, she felt a special personal attachment to him. But now his rancorous speeches and bullying ways made her realize that he was a flawed man. She read in the newspaper that Roosevelt called his opponent, Mr. Taft, a "fathead" and had the "brain of a guinea pig". Taft said Roosevelt followers were "radical" and "neurotic". When Theodore Roosevelt did not become the Republican party nominee, he formed a third party called the Bull Moose Party. Harriet Louise wanted to support Roosevelt because he was a proponent of women's suffrage, but she did not like his demeanor. This year she seriously considered changing her allegiance from Republican to Democrat and advocate for Mr. Woodrow Wilson who had the type of intellect and statesman like quality that Harriet Louise preferred. If only she could vote.

Harriet Louise received a letter from her nephew John Sidney Clark from Connecticut. He gave a grand account of how he was in the stadium and watched the final 1912 World Series baseball game between Boston and New York. He made it sound very exciting. Harriet Louise was not a big sports fan but she of course read about sports in the newspapers and knew about the famous World Series games. John also let Harriet Louise know that her sister, Mary Ellen, was doing well now, although it took some time for her to recover from her husband's death. John enclosed a photograph of the huge headstone monument where Mr. Clark was interred in Elm Grove Cemetery, Windsor, Hartford County, Connecticut. [204] John conveyed that his sisters, Fannie and Hattie, were okay as far as he knew. He said some day he wanted to visit Iowa and see his sister Eunice and his Aunt Susan, Aunt Harriet Louise and Uncle Peter Dewalt. Harriet Louise found it interesting that her nephew, John, wanted to come see her but there was no mention that her sister, Mary Ellen, wanted to come and see her. Well, probably because she didn't want to come see her. Mary Ellen was always the "absent" sister.

Another Christmas came and went. Florence and Harriet Louise attended a church service and an orchestra concert. They exchanged one gift to each other. They made dinner reservations at the Savery and ate more food in one sitting on Christmas evening than they had eaten the past week. The Savery was beautifully decorated and the pork packing plant was no longer in the basement. Downtown Des Moines was a burgeoning place of successful banking, finance and insurance businesses and many retail markets. Their family home on Locust was sold by the Barcroft-McCaughan Law and Real Estate firm to a property development company. Now a tall brick building

Mary Ellen Ankeny Clark
1839-1922

stood where their wood frame home with lovely gardens and fruit trees once stood. Somehow it did not sadden Harriet Louise. Her memories were vivid of the parties, events and conversations that took place in the home, but also the sorrows. Harriet Louise totally embraced progress. She was never the first to try something new, but once she understood and trusted the new inventions and conveniences, she was eager to move forward. Onward and upward was her favorite benediction.

Paul Lorah Ankeny caringly traveled with his elderly parents back to Iowa from Florida. Peter Dewalt wanted to be in Iowa in his final days. It took them five days to travel in their newly purchased Ford automobile. They stayed with Susan until Paul could find a suitable place for Peter and Ellen to rent. One day, while Paul and Ellen were out looking at apartments, Peter Dewalt and Harriet Louise spent the afternoon together. The brother and sister discussed everything under the sun. Peter was concerned with the growth of government. He never did like the USDA and now there would be another unnecessary government bureaucracy -- the Department of Labor.

He was never very emotional but he was outraged about these new expensive office buildings and how this new income tax system was seizing citizens' money to pay for these wasteful bureaucracies. When Harriet Louise agreed and mentioned the new Bureau of Fisheries, Peter Dewalt totally lost his temper. He said, "Imagine some college boy in some fancy suit telling me I can or can't fish or hunt on my own property." Harriet Louise decided it was time to change the subject. Harriet Louise said, "Well if women had the right to vote these atrocities would not be taking place." That seemed to calm down Peter. Actually, he was only quiet because he thought that statement was so ludicrous that it did not even deserve a response. And so the elderly brother and sister reminisced about Ohio and what they remembered of Millersburg. They talked about their parents, Joseph and Harriet Susanna. Harriet Louise was glad to be able to talk with her last living brother. She knew though that the next time she would avoid talking politics with Peter. His face grew too red and his hands too shaky and he was too old to be that agitated.

Peter's son, Paul Lorah Ankeny, was one of the kindest men Harriet Louise had ever known. He cared for his parents with such tenderness and concern. There was nothing he would not do for them. He was their only son. He had no wife or children. He was also very kind to Harriet Louise and engaged her in the most satisfying conversations about the new highway across America which would greatly improve safety for motorized traffic as well as speed up cross country travel. They talked about the Panama Canal completion. Paul Lorah said it will greatly help their fruit transportation to the west coast. He tried to explain the new assembly line factories in Detroit to Harriet Louise. He expressed a desire to someday work in a manufacturing plant with Henry Ford and that he was studying industrial management from the writings of Frank and Lillian Gilbreth. [205] They had great ideas for increasing production and therefore profits. This was all new to Harriet Louise. Harriet Louise said, "if I were your age I would study those business concepts with you Paul." Of course no conversation was complete until Harriet Louise brought up her pet subject of women's suffrage. Being the polite person he was, he agreed with Auntie Hattie.

Paul returned to Ankona, Florida where he owned and managed one of the largest fruit growing, canning and distributing companies in Florida. He left his parents in the guardianship of his Aunt Susan and Aunt Harriet Louise. Paul felt more comfortable with his two aunts looking after his parents than his own sisters. Peter and Ellen's youngest daughter, Mabel, had died in 1912. [206] Her husband, Mr. Matthews and their small daughter lived in Des Moines but he seemed too distant to care for Peter and Ellen. Mary Louise and George Burnett were living on the old farmstead and they also both worked at fulltime jobs in the city. [207] They seemed too busy to look after Peter and Ellen. Daisy and Mr. Green were doing very well in Des Moines. [208] When their late-in-life surprise child was born, they were consumed with her every breath. They were too preoccupied to give Peter and Ellen the care they needed. Rose Bonnet and Mr. Lewis were fulfilling their dream of living in Florida. [209] They truly were too distant to help with Peter and Ellen.

Paul and Harriet Louise made a pact that they would write each other often and maybe use the telephone on birthdays and holidays.

It was not a holiday, but Harriet Louise telephoned Paul in Florida. His father was gone. Peter Dewalt Ankeny was almost ninety years old when he passed away. All of his daughters, sons-in-law and families came together in Des Moines to prepare for the funeral and burial. Ellen was still strong and healthy. Peter's funeral was not nearly as big and full of circumstance as his parents' and brothers' funerals. A new funeral and burial service was utilized. When the family gathered at the funeral parlor and viewed the body of Peter Dewalt lying in a beautiful casket, they were amazed how similar he looked in death as he did in life.

It was really only Harriet Louise and Susan who knew the full life story of Peter Dewalt. The two sisters weren't known for public speaking but they were totally qualified to deliver the eulogy and conducting the funeral service for their brother. Together they delivered a stirring eulogy, they recited Bible passages, and the reading of Peter's descendants. Susan led hymns including a family favorite "This Is My Father's World, Why Should My Heart Be Sad". The funeral took place at the new funeral parlor.

Peter Dewalt Ankeny
1826-1915

Once again grandchildren and friends were surprised when they learned the full and most remarkable life of another Ankeny man. First Susan told the German history behind the name Dewalt and that Peter Dewalt Ankeny was born in Somerset County, Pennsylvania and moved with his three brothers and parents to Ohio when he was five years old. She told how he was educated in law at Kenyon College, was a Lieutenant in the Mexican War, came to Iowa and claimed land for the Ankeny family and met and married Ellen. His bravery, work ethic and unending search for a prosperous life led him and Ellen to go out west during Indian uprisings to gold mining territory where they lived in a primitive camp mining for gold and worked in saloons. They returned to Iowa after the war and put down roots near Berwick in Polk County, Iowa. Their land was near where John Fletcher and Joseph staked land claims. [210] [211] [212]

Now it was Harriet Louisa's turn and she told how Peter and Ellen had six children. Everyone thought they had five children. Harriet Louise explained how they lost their first little one out in the remote and untamed western territory which is now Colorado. Peter and Ellen resolved to not talk about her death and only remember her life. Harriet Louise gave a touching tribute to his children including their daughter Mabel who they lost only a few years ago. Paul and his three sisters all sat in the front row with their arms entwined at the elbows. Their stoic mother, Ellen Lorah Ankeny, sat straight and tall and dabbed tears from her eyes with a handkerchief embroidered with orange blossoms. The Ankeny families drove their motorized automobiles behind the beautiful long black hearse to Glendale Cemetery where Peter Dewalt was interred near his daughter, Mabel Ankeny Matthews. [213]

And now it was only Susan and Harriet Louise. It seemed that finally they could bear to be with each other. Age and years will do that. They talked about their sister Mary Ellen and they said they would go to Connecticut some day and see her. They knew it was just talk. Susan was doing well by herself in her new, small bungalow. Harriet Louise took Susan's advice and donated many of her parents' heirlooms to the Iowa Historical Society Museum. [214] The museum was just down the street on Grand. Florence's job at the Iowa Capitol Library put her in touch with the right people to make the donations. She worked with the archivist to describe and document the items. The process was enjoyable and reminded Harriet Louise of the work she performed for D.A.R. in Washington, D.C.

Susan Fletcher Ankeny Barcroft
1832-1916

It was April and the tulips, daffodils and hyacinths were in full bloom. The flowering trees were fully blossomed out. The air was warm with the promise of summer to come. Harriet Louise went to Susan's front door, knocked three times, opened the latch, and shouted her customary Yoo Hoo, Susan! As she entered, Harriet Louise, got that feeling she felt that April morning of her mother's death. Something was not right, not in place, not normal. Harriet Louise found her sister on the kitchen floor. She rang the telephone operator and asked her to dispatch a doctor or ambulance or something to 4155 Ingersoll Avenue. It seemed an eternity until help came. Harriet Louise sat down on the floor, next to her sister, took her still hands in hers, and cried quietly, and whispered, "I'm sorry Susan". Eternity. She contemplated what eternity would be like. Harriet Louise knew she, too, would know soon, her four brothers and two sisters and parents already knew.

Harriet Louise had lived a very full life and enjoyed life but she had a regret. A regret is reserved for when a person does not do the right thing and knows better. Harriet Louise regretted she had not treated her sister, Susan, with more kindness.

Susan's funeral was formal and small. The local Abigail Adams chapter of D.A.R. provided a luncheon afterwards down the street at the Iowa Historical Society Museum meeting room. Their kindness was for the deceased "daughter" Susan and for the living "daughter" Harriet Louise. Harriet Louise was warm and friendly to Susan's children and their families. Susan was, of course, interred at Woodland. [215] The new norms of burial allowed the burial to take place a day after the memorial funeral ceremony. And so the family assembled again at the funeral parlor. The director of the funeral establishment condescendingly reminded Harriet Louise that the motorcade could be for family only. He was looking around and saw many autos and lots of people. Harriet Louise raised her chin, looked down her nose and boldly said, "This IS family, we are the Ankenys."

Thank goodness Florence had learned to drive a motor car. Florence and Harriet Louise were going here and there and everywhere in their auto. They were able to make frequent trips to Adams County and up to Franklin

County. They drove to Iowa City for graduations. They could walk to their church on Sunday mornings, but they drove. Their walking and horse riding and carriage pulling days were gone for good. Both women agreed there was nothing good about the good old days.

When Florence was at work, Harriet Louise had to be patient at home and wait for her chauffeur to come home. Harriet Louise never learned to drive the auto. She thought she would have learned if younger, but what would be the point of learning to steer and then the next day be six feet under. She thought there was no point wasting anyone's time trying to teach her to steer that steel contraption.

Florence and Harriet Louise were getting quite the reputation around town. They were full of life and laughter for their age. They were smart and witty and fun to be with. They had a couple of male admirers but they were merely a source of amusement for Florence and Harriet Louise. They went out on double dates to the orchestra and dinners at the Savery. They laughed about how nice it was to enjoy a free meal.

One day they bought look-alike outfits. They started wearing the mid-calf dresses to events. They turned heads and created gossip and they liked stirring the pot.

Another fun adventure for them was to go to the Brown Hotel where Sue lived and worked with her very capable and handsome and now rich husband, Ernest Warren Brown. Their little boys were now young men and treated their Auntie Florence and Great Auntie Hattie with all kinds of special surprises in the hotel lobby. They played cards with the boys and agreed to chaperone parties at the hotel lobby for the young people.

As the young and old generations mingled with merriment, there was a serious and deadly war going on in Europe. Young men started arriving in Des Moines for training and the Savery and Brown establishments housed the young soldiers. Harriet and Florence volunteered at the Brown and served food. The charm and vivacious personalities of Florence and Harriet were entertaining to the young men. The women were good listeners. The soldiers told stories about their swimming lessons at the world's largest swimming pool at Camp Dodge. This was not recreational swimming though, it was water survival skills training in case their ship at sea was blown up, sunk or seized.

This was a frightening thought for Harriet Louise. Her great nephew, Robert Ankeny Brown a Second Class Seaman, was serving in the Navy and on a ship somewhere she did not know where. [216] Harriet Louise had to smile at the memory of Fletcher Ankeny Russell boasting that he would teach his cousin, little Bob, how to swim in Florida. And now, Bob a military man, had completed officer training school at the Culver Military Academy and was on a Navy ship in the middle of a vast ocean. Harriet mused, I am quite sure Bob is a good swimmer, and it is all because of Fletcher. Yes, indeed, the older Ankenys help the younger Ankenys and in ways and for reasons not known at the time but can be witnessed – if one lives long enough.

Harriet Louise had lived a long time. She lived through the Civil War. She stayed with her sisters-in-law as they managed their husbands' farms and survived bitter cold winters and buried children while their husbands were away. They endured not knowing if they would see their husbands again. Those years prepared them all for the future in some way and some form.

So when Harriet Louise read about the war and saw the young men in uniform at the Brown, she had flashbacks of the travesties of war. She wanted everyone to be happy and not suffer. Why could men not control their tempers and come to some sort of agreement. Why could they not compromise? Why did they always have to be right? Why couldn't women vote? If women could vote, there would be no more wars.

It was another happy homecoming when Robert Brown returned to Iowa and was placed in charge of officer training in Ames, Iowa. [217] He lived in barracks under the West Stadium on the Iowa State College campus.[218] One day Florence and Harriet had the hair- brained idea that they could just drive up to Ames and walk into those barracks and see Robert. When they arrived they were promptly turned away. The two women agreed that only men could make up such foolish rules.

Woodrow Wilson finally came around to supporting a federal women's suffrage amendment and at the end of World War I he made it a priority and addressed the U.S. Senate about an amendment. In August of 1920 three quarters of the state legislatures ratified the Nineteenth Amendment. American Women had won full voting rights. [219]

Harriet Louise was ecstatic. She shouted, "hip hip hooray!" but her shout was really only a whisper. Her stamina, voice and steadiness were diminishing. Her voice was raspy and at the end of a day she had no voice. She rested her voice and drank soothing teas and other elixirs. The newest fixer of all ills was sarsaparilla and she tried that too. She drank cool beverages, she drank hot beverages, nothing restored her voice.

When it was time to vote for President, Harriet Louise Ankeny and Florence Ankeny Russell were almost the first in line. Harriet Louise had, of course, read and studied all of the issues and had strong opinions about the character of the men running. Since the Civil War her family had voted as Lincoln Republicans. And so she would too. When it came time to vote, it seemed, she was following her brothers and father after all. She was not in favor of the Woodrow Wilson years of expanding government and interventionism. She liked that two Iowa men, Herbert Hoover and Henry Wallace supported Warren Harding. [220] She did not like that another Roosevelt, even if he was only a fifth cousin of Theodore, would be near the White House, and Franklin D Roosevelt was the Vice Presidential pick for Mr. Cox, the Democrat.

Mr. Harding won in a landslide in the first presidential election that women could vote. Harriet Louise hoped that Mr. Harding would do his women voters proud. Harriet would never really know. By Christmas time she was barely able to greet all of the visitors to Florence's home. She was tired and weak and her cough wore her out. The doctors said her condition was incurable. Some days were better than others and she took advantage of the good days to read the newspapers, bake a treat for Florence and sort through her many letters and travel souvenirs and personal items. She documented and stored them, and hoped Florence or someone would see to their safe keeping when she was gone. She had given away most of her fine jewelry. Her last will and testament was on file.

Florence helped Harriet Louise down the porch steps and up into the auto. They would take drives around Des Moines and reminisce about days gone by. Harriet remembered when the streets were lined with horses and carriages. Now the horses are all at the outskirts of town in stables or farms. She remembered when outdoor privies were in every backyard and now they were few and far between, in Des Moines anyway. They drove to Woodland and prayed at the Ankeny burial site where Harriet Louise would, soon she knew, be at rest. [221] They drove up north to Ankeny, the town named after their brother, John Fletcher Ankeny. It was a sleepy little town but the store, house and post office and hotel built by John Fletcher Ankeny were still there. They drove out past Peter's farm near Berwick. The home looked forlorn and in need of repair. Florence's own home on Grand was on the list of eminent domain conquests. State government and office buildings were going up everywhere to be near the Iowa Capitol Building and the Polk County and Federal Court Houses and City Hall. The Des Moines Public Library was a sanctuary for the two women. They often went there and just watched the people mill around, enjoying the lifeblood of the young people, the absorption of knowledge by the adults, and the understanding that it all contributed to a better Des Moines, Polk County, State of Iowa and United States. Harriet Louise cherished learning since her childhood. Like her ancestors before her, she passed on knowledge to the next generation. Harriet liked progress. Harriet Louise cherished the past, she learned from the past, but she did not hang onto it. Onward and upward.

Warren Bonnet Ankeny drove his mother, Tina, to Des Moines from Adams County to see Harriet Louise. Tina packed a suitcase and insisted on staying with Harriet Louise for a while. She wanted to be with Harriet Louise and also help Florence. It was many, many years ago, during the Civil War, Harriet Louise stayed with Tina on the farm while their brother and husband, Henry Giese Ankeny, was fighting in the war. Tina's life was not easy then. Tina always believed that she would not have survived those years, and one particularly severe case of pneumonia, had it not been for Harriet Louise by her side. Tina told anyone who would listen how wonderful Harriet Louise had been to her. Now Tina was going to try and repay her dear sister-in-law for her dedication. Tina sat near Harriet Louise and reminisced about those early days, the good and the bad times. Harriet Louise listened and nodded her head.

Florence knew she would not have her dear Aunt Hattie, her treasured companion, for very much longer. Harriet Louise made the best of every good day and endured the bad days. Harriet Louise lived to see the President she voted for sworn into office. When she saw the inauguration photo on the Des Moines Register front page, Harriet Louise wrote on a piece of her beautiful stationery, "I did that."

She did.

Descendants of Joseph and Harriet Ankeny

<hr/>

"A strong plant needs good seed.
A tall tree requires deep roots.
A future of promises for any people
rests upon a worthy past, worthily kept."

JOSEPH AND HARRIET HAD 8 Children, 33 Grandchildren, 49 Great Grand-children, 75 Second Great Grandchildren, 81 Third Great Grandchildren, 46 Fourth Great Grandchildren, and 8 Fifth Great Grandchildren for a total of 300 known descendants as of February 23, 2016. The following is a five-generation list of descendants.

1-Joseph A ANKENY (30 Jun 1802-9 May 1876)
+Harriet Susanna GIESE (Feb 1801-Apr 1897)

2-John Fletcher ANKENY (6 May 1824-9 Apr 1886)

+Sarah Hagar "Sally" WOLGAMOT (29 Nov 1829-1903)

3-Florence ANKENY (23 Nov 1858-14 Aug 1930)

+George Peter RUSSELL (1851-20 Jan 1879)

4-Fletcher Ankeny RUSSELL (9 Jan 1877-30 Dec 1968)

+Grace MOTT (11 May 1875-26 Jun 1957)

3-Mary Bird ANKENY (9 Jun 1860-17 Aug 1926)

+Benson Ehret ISRAEL (18 Mar 1854-1923)

4-William Dwight Israel DOLLISON (23 May 1886-Oct 1964)

+Laura MAXWELL (15 Aug 1887-Feb 1965)

5-William Chapin Israel DOLLISON (16 May 1919-Nov 1977)

5-Eleanor Ankeny ISRAEL (8 May 1922-10 Oct 1940)

5-Robert Benson Israel DOLLISON (2 Jun 1930-)

3-Harriet Giese ANKENY (28 Mar 1864-Mar 1957)

+Delos W MOTT (11 Nov 1832-29 Nov 1911)

3-Susan ANKENY (14 Aug 1867-14 Mar 1958)

+Ernest Warren BROWN (12 Jun 1867-6 May 1934)

4-Emerson Ankeny BROWN (1896-1897)

4-Robert Ankeny BROWN (26 Jun 1899-26 Nov 1976)

+Greta Huntington WEITZ (28 May 1903-21 Dec 1986)

5-Philip Ankeny BROWN (1 Aug 1928-12 Jun 2014)

5-Ernest Weitz BROWN (23 May 1933-17 Dec 2013)

2-Peter Dewalt ANKENY (3 Feb 1826-9 Oct 1915)

+Ellen LORAH (Jan 1839-1935)

3-ANKENY (15 Jul 1861-)

3-Rose Bonnet ANKENY (8 Feb 1865-20 May 1934)

+Thomas Edgar LEWIS (14 Jun 1868-15 Nov 1940)

4-Elizabeth LEWIS (Mar 1893-)

4-Edna A LEWIS (Sep 1896-)

+Frank MARSHALL (1882-)

3-Daisy ANKENY (Dec 1866-1967)

+Frank Owen GREEN (1862-23 Jun 1934)

4-Marjorie GREEN (26 Feb 1902-17 Sep 1991)

+Burton Forest BRISTOW (4 Oct 1899-31 May 1955)

5-John Barry BRISTOW (23 Feb 1927-3 May 1952)

5-Nancy Ankeny BRISTOW (1928-)

5-Elizabeth Hayes BRISTOW (1936-)

3-Mary Louise ANKENY (1869-1941)

+George Caleb BURNETT (1867-1948)

3-Paul Lorah ANKENY (10 Jun 1872-7 Oct 1965)

3-Mabel ANKENY (28 Mar 1879-13 Apr 1912)

+William Howard MATTHEWS (1881-)

4-Ellen Louise MATTHEWS (29 Mar 1908-)

2-Henry Giese ANKENY (24 Dec 1827-17 Mar 1906)

+Horatia Fostina "Tina" NEWCOMB (1841-1928)

3-Jessie ANKENY (24 Aug 1860-15 Sep 1861)

3-Joseph Newcomb ANKENY (29 Oct 1861-5 Mar 1949)

+Elma H ROGERS (6 Apr 1864-26 Feb 1953)

4-Jessie Valentine ANKENY (27 Dec 1883-10 Apr 1979)

+Henry Veere LACY (5 Oct 1886-23 Mar 1975)

5-Mary Nind LACY (1916-)

5-Henry Ankeny LACY (11 Sep 1917-3 Oct 2002)

5-Alice LACY (1922-)

5-Dorothy LACY (19 Feb 1924-19 Aug 2012)

4-Blanche ANKENY (31 Aug 1885-18 Jul 1913)

+Charles CHAPMAN (4 Nov 1881-25 Oct 1953)

4-Ralph Dewalt ANKENY (14 Oct 1887-May 1973)

+Ida M RHINE (1889-1946)

5-Pauline ANKENY (1 Jun 1908-9 May 1998)

5-Dorothy ANKENY (5 May 1910-30 May 2011)

5-Joseph Newcomb ANKENY (8 Sep 1914-26 Oct 2009)

5-Doris Maxine ANKENY (23 Sep 1916-20 Apr 1989)

5-Homer R ANKENY (12 Feb 1919-26 May 1990)

5-Shirley ANKENY (1934-)

4-Helen Lucile ANKENY (22 Oct 1891-25 May 1959)

+Emil Anthon JOHNSON (1888-21 Apr 1937)

5-Roger Ankeny JOHNSON (2 Dec 1914-1 Aug 1993)

5-Phillip Newcomb JOHNSON (10 Feb 1923-Nov 1973)

4-Homer R ANKENY (1894-Jun 1970)

+Rose C (28 Apr 1901-3 Jul 1967)

+Edith BROTT (30 Jun 1895-21 Mar 1925)

5-infant daughter ANKENY (16 Mar 1925-16 Mar 1925)

5-infant daughter ANKENY (16 Mar 1925-16 Mar 1925)

4-Harriet Louise ANKENY (3 Feb 1896-27 Dec 1989)

+Ralph W LITTLE (1895-1976)

4-Florence Marie ANKENY (7 Sep 1898-14 Jan 1991)

+Harold Herbert COX (1 Feb 1898-31 Oct 1987)

5-Harold Richard COX (8 Oct 1922-31 Mar 2011)

5-Barbara J COX (-)

5-Marilyn COX (-)

4-Henry Giese ANKENY (22 Oct 1900-14 Dec 1976)

+Irene DELANEY (17 Jul 1895-31 Jan 1990)

5-Margaret Louise ANKENY (20 Nov 1921-7 Jun 2007)

5-Jo Anne ANKENY (1924-)

5-Rita Irene ANKENY (1925-)

5-Virginia Ruth ANKENY (1928-)

3-Rosa ANKENY (9 Jun 1864-22 Aug 1864)

3-Warren Bonnet ANKENY (11 Feb 1866-1953)

+Osia JOSLYN (8 Apr 1870-1940)

4-Colin Clinton ANKENY (30 Apr 1895-19 Jun 1959)

+Irene STENWALL (1899-1 Jan 1981)

5-Colin Stenwall ANKENY Jr (20 May 1929-24 May 1998)

4-Faustina ANKENY (16 May 1900-Nov 1984)

+Paul O INGWERSEN (1890-1969)

5-C Bernhard INGWERSEN (11 Sep 1924-13 Dec 2007)

3-John Barcroft ANKENY (1 May 1867-10 Jun 1926)

+Louetta L DEVORE (18 Jul 1871-2 Oct 1930)

4-Chester Devore ANKENY (10 Apr 1891-16 May 1959)

+Grace Elinor HALL (8 May 1893-22 Nov 1983)

5-Lois Elizabeth ANKENY (22 Nov 1917-27 Sep 2004)

5-Ronald Ormel ANKENY (5 Dec 1920-10 Mar 2006)

5-Earl ANKENY (23 Sep 1922-13 Nov 1956)

5-Helen ANKENY (1925-)

4-Russell Barcroft ANKENY (19 Sep 1893-23 Dec 1988)

+Ida SHERMAN (19 Nov 1897-23 Nov 1987)

5-Ruthe L ANKENY (6 Nov 1917-2 Oct 2012)

5-John Isaiah ANKENY (21 Sep 1919-26 Sep 1985)

5-Roy Russell ANKENY (2 Jul 1922-20 Mar 1995)

5-Janet Bell ANKENY (1932-)

3-Henry G "Harry" ANKENY Jr (3 Apr 1870-6 May 1898)

+Emma CHAFFEE (24 Mar 1870-19 Aug 1957)

3-Rollin V ANKENY (27 Dec 1871-3 Aug 1956)

+Edythe M PEASE (1878-Nov 1961)

4-Harold R ANKENY (15 Mar 1901-31 Jan 1980)

+Ruth Frances WILLIS (1901-1948)

5-Rollin F ANKENY (1926-)

5-Barry David ANKENY (24 May 1932-8 Nov 2004)

+Eulalia "Lolly" HARRIS (1899-1979)

+Natalie Isabel HARLEY (1905-)

4-Barbara E ANKENY (1907-)

3-Dr Ralph L ANKENY (2 Jan 1874-2 Jun 1973)

+Janet Arnott YUILL (1878-)

4-Ralph Clement ANKENY (4 Jun 1907-23 Aug 1961)

+Sybil Elinor (19 Oct 1908-3 Jun 2008)

5-Joyce ANKENY (-)

5-Peter ANKENY (-)

3-Harriet Elizabeth ANKENY (2 Aug 1875-Sep 1967)

+Harold Horace HARRIS (11 May 1871-1946)

4-Fostina HARRIS (2 Jul 1906-20 Oct 1995)

+Louis Nelson HOOPLE (1900-1986)

5-Patricia Ann HOOPLE (5 Apr 1933-2 Apr 2005)

5-Betty L HOOPLE (1930-)

4-Arthur Ankeny HARRIS (20 Dec 1911-7 Jun 1983)

+Opal Ernestine "Jackie" HART (19 Jan 1917-31 Jul 2007)

5-Harold Hart HARRIS (1939-)

5-son HARRIS (-)

5-son HARRIS (-)

3-Ethel ANKENY (1 Feb 1882-6 May 1883)

2-Rollin Valentine ANKENY (22 May 1830-24 Dec 1901)

+Sarah IRVINE (1835-12 Jan 1879)

3-Irvine Sample ANKENY (1854-30 Sep 1886)

3-Harriet Louise ANKENY (20 Oct 1856-20 Jul 1889)

+John CONGER (1851-)

4-Rollin Valentine CONGER (9 May 1875-17 Dec 1887)

4-Edwin Hurd CONGER (17 Jul 1879-)

3-Joseph R "Josie" ANKENY (Sep 1859-12 Dec 1861)

3-Rollin Valentine ANKENY (1 Sep 1865-30 Oct 1934)

+Elinor "Nellie" RANDOLPH (1868-18 Nov 1947)

4-Irvine Randolph ANKENY (26 Jun 1891-7 Dec 1975)

+Genevieve SMITH (1893-Feb 1939)

5-Florence A ANKENY (8 Jul 1910-10 Dec 1955)

+Winifred HARKINS CAHEN (1889-1987)

3-Mary Bonnet ANKENY (1870-Jun 1955)

+Frederick Heaton HUNTER (7 Jun 1869-23 Jul 1943)

4-Leland Day HUNTER (27 Apr 1894-25 Dec 1966)

+Isabelle GRAY (1889-)

+Leondy C (1894-)

5-Berniece HUNTER (1915-)

5-Evelyn HUNTER (1920-)

4-Josephine HUNTER (1898-)

+Harvey T RAY (1894-)

4-Rollin Valentine HUNTER (1909-)

+Ruth D (-)

2-Susan Fletcher ANKENY (22 Jul 1832-Apr 1916)

+John Russell BARCROFT (13 May 1824-20 Jan 1901)

3-Mary Louise BARCROFT (5 Feb 1855-Jun 1946)

+George Elias KING (7 Jan 1846-25 Jan 1912)

4-Edith B KING (1 Sep 1879-Sep 1963)

+William W PEARSON (1870-)

+W W BELL (-)

4-Alice B KING (7 Aug 1881-13 Jun 1934)

+Frank Rhea BOTT (-)

5-Margaret King BOTT (9 Oct 1910-21 Jun 1934)

3-Harriet L "Hattie" BARCROFT (11 Jan 1857-Jun 1921)

+James McCullough MCCAUGHAN (1853-1900)

4-John Barcroft MCCAUGHAN (28 Mar 1877-2 Sep 1960)

+Amelia TALCOTT (28 Nov 1888-27 Jul 1974)

5-Norton J MCCAUGHAN (14 Apr 1913-27 Dec 2005)

5-Fletcher B MCCAUGHAN (19 Mar 1916-27 Apr 2008)

5-Mary MCCAUGHAN (5 Oct 1918-8 Feb 1998)

5-Harriet Avis MCCAUGHAN (7 Aug 1924-16 Jun 2007)

4-Susie E MCCAUGHAN (1879-1880)

4-Ralph L MCCAUGHAN (26 Aug 1881-19 Jul 1975)

+Dorothy Eva MANBECK (1885-)

5-James Russell MCCAUGHAN (18 Jun 1907-27 May 2000)

5-Roland Geil MCCAUGHAN (30 Aug 1908-2 Oct 1984)

5-Barbara MCCAUGHAN (1912-)

5-R Lewis MCCAUGHAN (1917-)

4-George Louis MCCAUGHAN (20 Nov 1884-Dec 1969)

+Emma Belle MILLER (1888-1964)

5-Dwight Lewis MCCAUGHAN (1 Feb 1908-6 Sep 1922)

5-Louise Ankeny MCCAUGHAN (17 Aug 1909-8 Dec 1980)

5-George Louis MCCAUGHAN Jr (1909-1910)

5-Rosie MCCAUGHAN (1910-1911)

5-Susan Jane MCCAUGHAN (26 May 1917-15 Aug 2001)

4-Louise Ankeny MCCAUGHAN (Dec 1888-Jul 1991)

+Otis Winfield PRAY (1885-1967)

5-William Pearson PRAY (24 Jun 1909-25 May 1999)

5-Eli Barcroft "Barry" PRAY (25 Jun 1912-19 Dec 1988)

5-James McCaughan PRAY (4 Apr 1915-1 Mar 1916)

5-Winfield Ankeny PRAY (9 Feb 1919-15 Jan 1991)

5-David R PRAY (27 Jan 1925-6 Mar 2011)

3-Russell Ankeny BARCROFT (8 Mar 1861-)

+Mary WRIGHT MINEAR (29 Apr 1864-)

+Fredericka STRASBURGER (1888-)

4-Russell A BARCROFT (15 Nov 1921-29 Apr 1991)

3-Joseph Kinsey BARCROFT (7 Aug 1865-28 Sep 1946)

+Harriet Etta COZENS (6 Jun 1875-)

4-Bazzelle B BARCROFT (3 Aug 1901-15 Nov 1984)

+Henry TAYLOR (1903-)

5-Henry D TAYLOR (1929-)

5-Josephine B TAYLOR (1931-)

2-Rosina Bonnet ANKENY (1 Sep 1835-24 Dec 1842)

2-Mary Ellen ANKENY (12 Jul 1839-19 Sep 1922)

+Henry Horton CLARK (24 Aug 1834-15 Feb 1893)

3-Eunice Aurelia CLARK (13 Sep 1861-15 Dec 1961)

+Webb SOUERS (22 Jul 1857-10 Nov 1926)

4-Henry Clark SOUERS (8 Aug 1888-Jul 1970)

+Dorothy FINKBINE (2 Dec 1894-8 Apr 1935)

5-William Clark SOUERS (6 Mar 1927-16 Oct 2009)

+Edith (-)

4-Marshall Ankeny SOUERS (1891-1957)

+Mildred THOMSON (26 Feb 1894-Aug 1977)

5-Marshall Ankeny SOUERS Jr (6 Dec 1920-11 Sep 2006)

4-Philip Webster SOUERS (6 Jan 1897-27 Sep 1957)

+Helen ORTON (1900-)

5-son SOUERS (-)

3-Harriet Ankeny "Hattie" CLARK (15 Sep 1863-3 Sep 1951)

+Charles Morgan HERO (1861-11 Oct 1941)

3-Frances Louise "Fannie" CLARK (11 Mar 1866-23 May 1956)

+Charles Dexter ALLEN (8 May 1865-10 Sep 1926)

4-Sylvia Mary ALLEN (10 May 1892-22 Apr 1962)

4-Louise Pierson ALLEN (10 Oct 1893-15 Apr 1897)

4-Marian ALLEN (10 Mar 1896-2 Mar 1907)

4-Barbara ALLEN (1 Sep 1901-)

3-John Sidney CLARK (7 Feb 1869-)

+Florence Adel Lane (27 Sep 1877-)

4-Florence CLARK (3 Jan 1897-)

4-Margarey CLARK (1 Jun 1898-)

2-Harriet Louise ANKENY (20 Nov 1844-19 May 1921)

Author's Message

———— ⌘ ————

My interest in genealogy started when my husband's Aunt Dot gave us a huge binder full of family history for Christmas. That inspired me to start poking around to find my own roots. My fascination with the Ankeny family started when my poking revealed I was related to the founder of the town, Ankeny, Iowa. I am the fifth great granddaughter of Dewalt Ankeny. The more I discovered about the Ankeny family the more intrigued I became. So I began researching and writing about this remarkable family.

Historical and Ankeny family information comes from many sources which I list in the Endnotes. The bulk of information comes from three main sources. 1) the thoroughly researched and excellent writings of Mr. Johnson Brigham (1846-1936) who was a noted author and historian and served as the State Librarian for Iowa for many years; 2) the Ankeny family Bibles, artifacts and letters that were donated and now stored at the State Historical Society of Iowa; and 3) the letters of Henry Giese Ankeny, written during the Civil War, which were compiled together and published in the book entitled "Kiss Josey For Me" in 1974 by Florence Marie Ankeny Cox.

I have used quotes in this book two ways. If quoted items are followed with an endnote notation there is a resource to support a fact. If quoted items do not include an endnote then it is a fictional conversation I have created to tell a story.

Thank you Jan Neal, my first cousin, for listening to me and accompanying me to the Iowa Museum and Archives to find Ankeny artifacts. Thank you Katharine Coats, Historical Program Specialist, Iowa Historical Society, for collecting and displaying many archived Ankeny artifacts for me to photograph. Thank you Janet Cox Armstrong, my sixth cousin, for becoming my friend and sounding board. Thank you Susan Hilary Brown for your generous time and allowing me access to numerous Ankeny photographs and documents. Thank you Cynde Keating and Todd Brown for meeting with me and showing me wonderful Ankeny photographs and sharing wonderful Ankeny memories. Thank you Jo Ankeny Lindamood for your Ankeny family insights.

I have enjoyed developing this story and connecting with descendants of Joseph and Harriet Ankeny. My original purpose was just personal enjoyment but as I learned more I was compelled (some say obsessed) to memorialize the Ankeny legacy. I also wanted to show the connection between the Chorpenning and Ankeny families. A secondary objective emerged as my curiosity about Miss Harriet Louise Ankeny and my imagination about her life would not subside. I decided to interpret the feelings, beliefs, thoughts and passions of an American woman about herself, her family, her God, her home.

ABOUT THE AUTHOR
Karla Wright is a retired Human Resource Management Consultant with a passion for family history and genealogy. This is Karla's first attempt at writing a fiction novel. Karla is a member of the Daughters of the American Revolution, the Honorary Order of the Society of the Bush Maryland Signers of 1775 Declaration of Independence, Ankeny Iowa Genealogy Chapter, Iowa Genealogical Society, Des Moines Historical Society and State Historical Society of Iowa.

ABOUT THE ILLUSTRATOR
Nathan T Wright is a digital marketing professional by day and an artist — illustrator by night. His work can be viewed at NathanTWright.com. Nathan captured so well the personalities of the Ankeny family members in their eyes. You can see sadness and happiness, pride and determination, and kindness and love in their eyes.

TIMELINE PHOTOGRAPHS

Memorial Marker for Dewalt Ankeny at St Paul's Lutheran Church Cemetery in Clear Spring, Maryland. Dewalt Ankeny left Germany and came to America in 1746. The inscription reads: TO THE MEMORY OF DEWALT ANKENY THE FIRST OF HIS NAME AND THE FOUNDER OF THAT FAMILY IN AMERICA. Dewalt is the Great Grandfather of Miss Harriet Louise Ankeny. Photograph by Matthew J Bridges and posted on FindAGrave.com memorial #37592033.

Ankeny Square Burial Ground is located in Somerset, Pennsylvania. Peter Ankeny was a founder of Somerset, was a Revolutionary War Patriot and donated the land for Ankeny Square. Peter Ankeny and his wife Rosina Bonnet are interred in Ankeny Square. Peter was the Father of Joseph and Grandfather of Miss Harriet Louise Ankeny. Photographed by Karla Wright, May 2014.

Two well preserved oil on ivory portraits of Joseph Ankeny (1802-1876) and Harriet Susanna Giese Ankeny (1801-1897) in leather cases were donated by Miss Harriet Louise Ankeny (their daughter) to the State Historical Museum of Iowa in 1911. Photographed by Karla Wright, April 2015.

Three Ankeny family Bibles were donated by Miss Harriet Louise Ankeny
to the State Historical Museum of Iowa in 1911. The very large Bible has
leather covers and closure, metal corners and many elaborate illustrations.
It was printed in 1765 in German. The medium sized New Testament Bible
was printed in 1835 and contains family records. The small Martin Luther's
New Testament Bible is printed in German in 1807. These Bibles traveled
with the Ankeny family from Somerset County, Pennsylvania to Millersburg,
Ohio to Des Moines, Iowa. Photographed by Karla Wright, June 12, 2015.

THE NEW YORK CRYSTAL PALACE.

The Crystal Palace in New York was constructed in 1853 from iron and glass as part of an All-Nations Exhibition. After the exhibition was over, the Crystal Palace remained open to visitors and was managed by P. T. Barnum. Joseph and Harriet Ankeny of Millersburg, Ohio traveled to New York City and visited the Crystal Palace. When they returned to Ohio they hosted friends and family and gave descriptive accounts of their travels to New York and especially the Crystal Palace. One particular noteworthy story Joseph told was about utilizing the newly designed and sophisticated indoor toilet within the Crystal Palace. It cost a penny to use the rest facility. Hence, the idiom "I'm going to spend a penny" came to be used when people politely removed themselves to use a rest facility

Civil War Sword of Henry Giese Ankeny, the third son of Joseph and
Harriet Ankeny. Henry joined Company H, Fourth Iowa Infantry at the
outbreak of the Civil War. He was appointed first lieutenant, was promoted
to captain, he was tendered the promotion of major but refused because
he promised to not abandon his youthful Adams County Iowa recruits.
He participated in twenty-eight engagements, including PeaRidge,
Lookout Mountain, Chickamauga and Vicksburg. In 2008 this
sword was donated (catalog number 2008.063.12) to the Iowa
Historical Society by Jo Ankeny Lindamood and Peter Ankeny.

Civil War Cap was donated by Miss Harriet Louise Ankeny to the State
Historical Museum of Iowa. This cap was worn by Orderly Sergeant
Major William (Billy) Wiggins of the Ohio Volunteers. He was from
Millersburg, Ohio and died at the Battle of Winchester, Virginia in 1862
when he was 23 years old. Photographed by Karla Wright, on February
23, 2016, at the State Historical Museum of Iowa, Des Moines, Iowa.

Covered wagons passed through downtown Des Moines before and during the Civil War. John Russell and Susan Ankeny Barcroft came to Iowa from Ohio in covered wagons in 1864. Susan was the daughter of Joseph and Harriet Ankeny. Mr. Barcroft was a prominent attorney in Des Moines. Photo from Des Moines Public Library Special Collections.

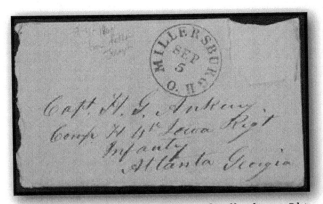

Envelope for a letter from Joseph Ankeny of Millersburg, Ohio, to his son Captain Henry Giese Ankeny while Henry was serving in the Union Army near Atlanta, Georgia in 1864. Henry Giese Ankeny Papers 1855-1919, Special Collections, State Historical Society of Iowa. Donated by Jo Ankeny Lindamood and Peter Ankeny, the Great Grandchildren of Henry Giese Ankeny. Photographed by Karla Wright, on November 21, 2015, at the State Historical Museum of Iowa, Des Moines, Iowa.

Photograph of Joseph A Ankeny, supplied by Susan Hilary Brown, Third Great Granddaughter of Joseph Ankeny.

Josephine Chorpenning Barron and her husband, David and four of her six children, circa 1880. Josephine and Harriet Louise Ankeny were Second Cousins Once Removed. The Ankeny and Chorpenning families were from Somerset County, Pennsylvania. David and Josephine moved to Black Hawk County, Iowa. Photograph supplied by Karla Wright.

Portrait of Harriet Giese Ankeny (Mrs. Joseph) by Jerome S. Uhl. Mrs.
Ankeny was born in Pennsylvania in 1801, moved to Ohio and then to
Iowa with her husband, and died in Des Moines in 1897. The large and
exquisite portrait measures 29" x 25" and is within a majestic golden frame.
The portrait hung on the wall of the State Library for many years but is
now stored inside a glass and wooden display case at the State Historical
Museum of Iowa. Photographed by Karla Wright, April 2015.

The original Iowa State Historical, Memorial and Art Building was built on 1110 East Grand Avenue. The cornerstone was laid in 1899. It was reported that 10,000 attended the ceremony which included a caravan of dignitaries in horse and carriages that paraded to the construction site down Grand Avenue from the Savery House. The building had wings and additions built in 1910 and later underwent an historic renovation and became the State Library of Iowa and renamed the Ola Babcock Miller Building. The collections, including the over one hundred Ankeny family artifacts donated by Harriet Louise Ankeny, were moved to the new Iowa State Historical Museum in 1987 now located at 600 East Locust Street. Photo from Des Moines Public Library Special Collections.

Photo of The Ankeny Clan circa 1896. Photograph supplied by L. Pray, the Third Great Grandchild of Joseph and Harriet Ankeny and Second Great Grandchild of Susan Fletcher Ankeny Barcroft. A similar photo appears in "Images of Des Moines 1845-1920" page 108. Many pioneers gathered together at the semicentennial of Des Moines in 1896. Harriet Susanna Giese Ankeny appears in this photo, second from the right, middle row. Harriet died in 1897.

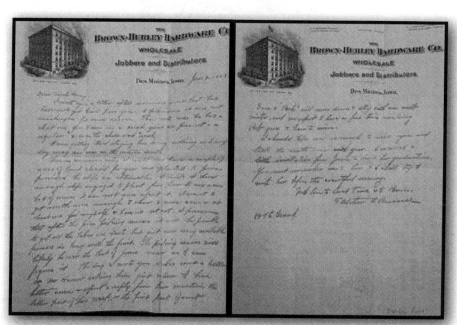

Letter from Fletcher Ankeny Russell to his Great Uncle Henry Giese
Ankeny seeking his support for growing pineapples in Florida in 1903.
This letter shows Fletcher living at 824 East Grand and using letterhead
from the business owned by his Uncle Ernest Brown. This is one of
many original letters found in the Henry Giese Ankeny Papers 1855-
1919, Special Collections, State Historical Society of Iowa, donated by Jo
Ankeny Lindamood and Peter Ankeny, the Great Grandchildren of Henry
Giese Ankeny in 2008. Photographed by Karla Wright, on November
21, 2015, at the State Historical Museum of Iowa, Des Moines, Iowa.

Anna Elizabeth Barron married John Henry Rigdon in 1903 in Black Hawk County, Iowa. Anna was born in 1881 to Josephine Chorpenning and David Barron. Anna's mother, Josephine, was a Second Cousin Once Removed with Harriet Louise Ankeny. Photograph supplied by Karla Wright.

Downtown Des Moines in 1910 was a busy and somewhat chaotic place. Street cars, horse and buggies and automobiles coexisted on the same streets. Photo from Des Moines Public Library Special Collections.

Ankeny Family Quilt was donated by Judy and Ernest Weitz Brown of Winterset to the Ankeny Area Historical Society Museum on Third Street in Ankeny, Iowa. The quilt is believed to be made by Harriet Giese Ankeny, John Fletcher Ankeny and Harriet Giese Ankeny Mott. The pieced squares are "Old Maid's Puzzle" pattern and the quilted squares are in the "Feathered Circle" design and the border pattern is "Double X". John Fletcher Ankeny founded the town of Ankeny in 1875 and he is the Great Grandfather of Ernest Weitz Brown. Photographed by Karla Wright in May of 2015.

In 1908 over one hundred brave women marched in Boone, Iowa in support of women's suffrage. Photograph from Women's Suffrage in Iowa Online Exhibit, University of Iowa Library.

The Brown Hotel was built in 1911in downtown Des Moines by Ernest Warren
Brown. Mr. Brown was married to Susan Ankeny the fourth daughter of
John Fletcher and Sarah Ankeny. The building was first used as a boarding
house. Within the Brown Hotel the Brown Marine Museum was created and
consisted of many mounted deep-sea specimens and featured well-known
and rare game fish from around the world caught by the Brown family on
their many deep sea fishing expeditions. Robert "Bob" Ankeny Brown, son
of Ernest and Susan Brown, managed and lived in the Brown Hotel with his
wife Greta Weitz. In 1975 Robert and Greta Brown narrated the history of
the Brown Hotel and provide Ankeny family anecdotes. The audio recording
can be found in the "Iowa Oral History Project" Des Moines Public Library.

ENDNOTES

1. Iowa: Its History and Its Foremost Citizens, Volume III, Johnson Brigham, 1918, Pages 1148 to 1157.

2. Des Moines: The Pioneer of Municipal Progress and Reform of the Middle West Together with the History of Polk County Iowa the Largest, Most Populous and Most Prosperous County in the State of Iowa, Johnson Brigham, 1911, Pages 626 to 634.

3. FindAGrave.com, Memorial #35927175, Harriet Louise Ankeny.

4. The Annals of Iowa, "That Our Memory May Be Green", Volume 24, Number 2, Fall 1942, Page 104.

5. Des Moines: The Pioneer of Municipal Progress and Reform of the Middle West Together with the History of Polk County Iowa the Largest, Most Populous and Most Prosperous County in the State of Iowa, Johnson Brigham, 1911, Pages 626 to 634.

6. Iowa: Its History and Its Foremost Citizens, Volume II, Johnson Brigham, 1918. Pages 52 to 55.

7. Des Moines: The Pioneer of Municipal Progress and Reform of the Middle West Together with the History of Polk County Iowa the Largest, Most Populous and Most Prosperous County in the State of Iowa, Johnson Brigham, 1911, Pages 626 to 634.

8. Sketch of the Life and Some of the Descendants of Dewald Ankeny, Charles Ross Shultz, 1948.

9. US and Canada Passenger and Immigration Lists Index 1500 to 1900, Ancestry.com.

10. Pennsylvania German Pioneers, Volume I and II, Strassburger and Hinke, 1980.

11. Publication of the Original Lists of Arrivals in the Port of Philadelphia from 1727 to 1808.

12. D A R, Daughters of the American Revolution documentation, Patriot #A002824.

13. Will of a Wealthy American in 1781, Washington County Maryland, Dewalt Ankeny, Ancestry.com.

14. FindAGrave.com, Memorial #37592033, Dewalt Ankeny.

15. Abstract of Graves of Revolutionary Patriots, Volume: 1; Serial: 11587; Volume: 4.

16. US and International Marriage Records 1560 - 1900, Ancestry.com.

17. S A R, Sons of the American Revolution documentation, Member #57277.

18. Heritage of Anna Elizabeth Barron Rigdon, 2014, Karla Rigdon Wright.

19. Sketch of the Life and Some of the Descendants of Dewald Ankeny, Charles Ross Shultz, 1948.

20. FindAGrave.com, Memorial #27989504, Ankeny Square Burial Ground, Captain Peter Ankeny.

21. FindAGrave.com, Memorial #32681945, Ankeny Square Burial Ground, Rosina Bonnet Ankeny.

22. Abstract of Graves of Revolutionary Patriots, Volume: 1; Serial: 12260; Volume: 5.

23. D A R, Daughters of the American Revolution documentation, Patriot #A002826.

24. Prominent Iowans, 1916, Johnson Brigham.

25. Iowa: Its History and Its Foremost Citizens, 1918, Johnson Brigham.

26. 1830 US Census, Somerset, Somerset, Pennsylvania, Joseph and Harriet Ankeny.

27. 1850 US Census, Hardy, Holmes, Ohio, Joseph and Harriet Ankeny.

28. 1860 US Census, Hardy, Holmes, Ohio, Joseph and Harriet Ankeny.

29. S A R, Sons of the American Revolution documentation, Member # 20993.

30. A Memorial and Biographical Record of Iowa, Illustrated, Volume II, 1896, Page 1154.

31. Hawkeye Heritage, Iowa Genealogical Society Newsletter, #23, Winter 1988, transcribed hand written family records from Joseph Ankeny Bible, Pages 220 to 223.

32. 1850 US Census, Sacramento, Sacramento, California, John Fletcher Ankeny.

33. Iowa: Its History and Its Foremost Citizens, Volume III, Johnson Brigham, 1918, pages 1148 to 1157.

34. US School Catalogs 1765-1935, Kenyon College, 1853.

35. Iowa: Its History and Its Foremost Citizens, Volume III, Johnson Brigham, 1918, pages 1148 to 1157.

36. US Mexican War Pension Index, Peter Dewalt Ankeny, 1888, Washington, D.C.

37. Iowa: Its History and Its Foremost Citizens, 1918, by Johnson Brigham.

38. 1850 US Census, Sacramento, Sacramento, California, Henry Giese Ankeny.

39. 1850 US Census, Hardy, Holmes, Ohio, Rollin Valentine Ankeny.

40. US School Catalogs 1765-1935, Western Reserve College, Ohio. 1853, Page 9.

41. Iowa: Its History and Its Foremost Citizens, 1918, by Johnson Brigham.

42. Des Moines: The Pioneer of Municipal Progress and Reform of the Middle West Together with the History of Polk County Iowa the Largest, Most Populous and Most Prosperous County in the State of Iowa, Johnson Brigham, 1911.

43. Heritage of Anna Elizabeth Barron Rigdon, 2014, Karla Rigdon Wright.

44. FindAGrave.com, Memorial #37397272, Framy Shaff Chorpenning.

45. FindAGrave.com, Memorial #65866405, Rosina Bonnet Ankeny, Engraved Prayer on Memorial.

46. S A R, Sons of the American Revolution documentation, Member #59541.

47. 1850 and 1860 US Census, Somerset, Somerset County, Pennsylvania, families of David Barron and families of Josephine Chorpenning.

48. Nicholas Barron Family History 1731-1994, Somerset, Pennsylvania.

49. The 200 Years of History of Samuel's Church, Somerset, Pennsylvania, from The History of Somerset, Bedford, and Fulton Counties, Pennsylvania 1884.

50. The Invention of Wings, 2014, history of abolitionist Grimke sisters, Sue Monk Kidd.

51. Uncle Tom's Cabin, 1852, Harriet Beecher Stowe.

52. Ain't I a Woman? 1851, Sojourner Truth.

53. 1860 US Census, Florence, Stephenson, Illinois, Sarah and Rollin Valentine Ankeny.

54. 1860 US Census, Florence, Stephenson, Illinois, Sally and John Fletcher Ankeny.

55. Gold Hill Museum, Boulder, Colorado, goldhillmuseum.org.

56. 1860 US Census, The Gold Hill Settlement, Shorter, Nebraska Territory, United States, Ellen and Peter Dewalt Ankeny.

57. 1860 US Census, Quincy, Adams, Iowa, Fostina and Henry Giese Ankeny.

58. 1860 US Census, Millersburg, Holmes, Ohio, Susan and John Russell Barcroft.

59. Iowa: Its History and Its Foremost Citizens, 1918, Johnson Brigham.

60. Iowa: Its History and Its Foremost Citizens, 1918, Johnson Brigham.

61. Iowa: Its History and Its Foremost Citizens, 1918, Johnson Brigham.

62. 1860 US Census, The Gold Hill Settlement, Shorter, Nebraska Territory, Peter Dewalt Ankeny.

63. Gold Hill Museum, Boulder, Colorado, goldhillmuseum.org.

64. Henry Giese Ankeny Papers, 1855-1919, MS2008.16, Special Collections, State Historical Society of Iowa, Des Moines, Iowa.

65. US Civil War Soldier Records and Profiles, Illinois: Roster of Officers and Enlisted Men, Heitman: Register of United States Army 1789-1903, National Archives: Index to Federal Pension Records, Dyer: A Compendium of the War of the Rebellion Brevet Brigadier Generals in Blue.

66. Civil War, Company H Fourth Iowa, posted 2013, iagenweb.org.

67. Kiss Josey For Me, Collection of Henry Giese Ankeny Civil War Letters, Florence Marie Ankeny Cox, 1974, Page 10.

68. Richard Cox, Second Great Grandson of Henry Giese Ankeny, email correspondence with Karla Wright, November 2015.

69. Kiss Josey For Me, Collection of Henry Giese Ankeny Civil War Letters, Florence Marie Ankeny Cox, 1974, Page 27.

70. FindAGrave.com, Memorial #40865192, Jessie Ankeny.

71. Kiss Josey For Me, Collection of Henry Giese Ankeny Civil War Letters, Florence Marie Ankeny Cox, 1974, Page 31.

72. Henry Giese Ankeny Papers, 1855-1919, MS2008.16, Special Collections, State Historical Society of Iowa, Des Moines, Iowa.

73. 1870 US Census, Quincy, Adams, Iowa, Joseph Newcomb Ankeny.

74. FindAGrave.com, Memorial #152149362, Joseph R "Josie" Ankeny.

75. Kiss Josey For Me, Collection of Henry Giese Ankeny Civil War Letters, Florence Marie Ankeny Cox, 1974, Page 88.

76. Henry Giese Ankeny Papers, 1855-1919, MS2008.16, Special Collections, State Historical Society of Iowa, Des Moines, Iowa.

77. FindAGrave.com, Memorial #119544268, William J Wiggins.

78. Civil War Cap worn by William (Billy) Wiggins, Catalog Number U01107, Iowa Historical Society Library and Archives.

79. FindAGrave.com, Memorial #119544268, Oak Hill Cemetery, Millersburg, Holmes County, Ohio.

80. Kiss Josey For Me, Collection of Henry Giese Ankeny Civil War Letters, Florence Marie Ankeny Cox, 1974, Page 94.

81. Kiss Josey For Me, Collection of Henry Giese Ankeny Civil War Letters, Florence Marie Ankeny Cox, 1974, Page 100.

82. Kiss Josey For Me, Collection of Henry Giese Ankeny Civil War Letters, Florence Marie Ankeny Cox, 1974, Page 110.

83. Kiss Josey For Me, Collection of Henry Giese Ankeny Civil War Letters, Florence Marie Ankeny Cox, 1974, Page 116.

84. Kiss Josey For Me, Collection of Henry Giese Ankeny Civil War Letters, Florence Marie Ankeny Cox, 1974, Page 152.

85. Kiss Josey For Me, Collection of Henry Giese Ankeny Civil War Letters, Florence Marie Ankeny Cox, 1974, Page 154.

86. Kiss Josey For Me, Collection of Henry Giese Ankeny Civil War Letters, Florence Marie Ankeny Cox, 1974, Page 165.

87. Kiss Josey For Me, Collection of Henry Giese Ankeny Civil War Letters, Florence Marie Ankeny Cox, 1974, Page 190.

88. Kiss Josey For Me, Collection of Henry Giese Ankeny Civil War Letters, Florence Marie Ankeny Cox, 1974, Page 193.

89. Iowa: Its History and Its Foremost Citizens, 1918, Johnson Brigham.

90. FindAGrave.com, Memorial #40865202, Rosa Ankeny.

91. Kiss Josey For Me, Collection of Henry Giese Ankeny Civil War Letters, Florence Marie Ankeny Cox, 1974, Page 240.

92. A Memorial and Biographical Record of Iowa, Illustrated, Volume II, 1896, Page 1154, General Rollin V. Ankeny.

93. American Civil War General Officers, Historical Data Systems, Ancestry.com, 1999.

94. Iowa: Its History and Its Foremost Citizens, 1918, by Johnson Brigham.

95. Kiss Josey For Me, Collection of Henry Giese Ankeny Civil War Letters, 1974, Page 214.

96. Ankeny Family Bibles, 1) New Testament 1835 (contains hand written family records) Call #220 B47 A63; 2) Martin Luther New Testament 1807 Call #220 B47 An61; 3) German Old and New Testament with Illustrations 1765 Call #220 B47 An63, Research Center, Iowa Historical Society Library and Archives.

97. Hawkeye Heritage, Iowa Genealogical Society Newsletter, #23, Winter 1988, transcribed hand written family records from Joseph Ankeny Bible, Pages 220 to 223.

98. Ankeny Family Bibles, 1) New Testament 1835 (contains hand written family records) Call #220 B47 A63; 2) Martin Luther New Testament 1807 Call #220 B47 An61; 3) German Old and New Testament with Illustrations 1765 Call #220 B47 An63, Research Center, Iowa Historical Society Library and Archives.

99. Sketch of the Life and Some of the Descendants of Dewald Ankeny, Charles Ross Shultz, 1948.

100. 1870 US Census, Des Moines, Polk County, Iowa, John Russell and Susan Barcroft, Joseph and Harriet S Ankeny, Harriet L Ankeny.

101. Iowa: Its History and Its Foremost Citizens, Johnson Brigham, 1918, John Russell Barcroft, pages 52to 55.

102. Iowa: Its History and Its Foremost Citizens, Johnson Brigham, 1918, John Russell Barcroft, pages 52to 55.

103. 1870 US Census, Polk City, Madison Township, Polk County, Iowa, Peter Dewalt and Ellen Ankeny.

104. 1870 US Census, Des Moines Ward 5, Polk County, Iowa, John Fletcher and Sally Ankeny.

105. Ankeny: The First One Hundred Years, Ankeny Historical Society, May 1993.

106. City Directory, Des Moines, Iowa, 1877, Page 133.

107. Images of America - Ankeny, Terri Deems with the Ankeny Area Historical Society, 2013.

108. Iowa: Its History and Its Foremost Citizens, 1918, by Johnson Brigham.

109. Ankeny: The First One Hundred Years, Ankeny Historical Society, May 1993.

110. Des Moines: The Pioneer of Municipal Progress and Reform of the Middle West Together with the History of Polk County Iowa the Largest, Most Populous and Most Prosperous County in the State of Iowa, Johnson Brigham, 1911, Pages 626 to 634.

111. American Civil War General Officers, Historical Data Systems, Ancestry.com, 1999.

112. Ankeny: The First One Hundred Years, Ankeny Historical Society, May 1993, Pages 18 and 19.

113. Iowa: Its History and Its Foremost Citizens, 1918, by Johnson Brigham.

114. Images of America - Ankeny, Terri Deems with the Ankeny Area Historical Society, 2013.

115. City Directory, Des Moines, Iowa, 1877, Page 133.

116. Wikipedia.org, Rollin V Ankeny.

117. Obituary for General Rollin V Ankeny, Adams County Free Press, Corning, Iowa, January 1902.

118. Obituary for General Rollin V Ankeny, The Des Moines Leader, Des Moines, Iowa, December 25, 1901.

119. The Annals of Iowa, Iowa and the Centennial Exhibition of 1876, Homer L. Calkin, Volume 43, Number 6, Fall 1976, Pages 443 – 458.

120. Biographical Directory of the United States Congress, Edwin Hurd Conger, bioguide.congress.gov.

121. Joseph Ankeny Descendants List, 2016, RootsMagic Database, Karla Rigdon Wright.

122. FindAGrave.com, Memorial #35927166, Joseph Ankeny.

123. 1880 US Census, Hartford, Hartford, Connecticut, Mary Ellen and Henry Clark.

124. 1900 US Census, Des Moines, Polk, Iowa, Eunice and Webb Souers.

125. 1880 US Census, East Waterloo, Black Hawk, Iowa, Josephine and David Barron.

126. Heritage of Anna Elizabeth Barron Rigdon, 2014, Karla Rigdon Wright.

127. Portrait of Harriet Susanna Giese Ankeny, painted by artist Jerome S. Uhl, Catalog Number 00032, Iowa Historical Library and Archives.

128. Ankeny Family Bibles, 1) New Testament 1835 (contains hand written family records) Call #220 B47 A63; 2) Martin Luther New Testament

1807 Call #220 B47 An61; 3) German Old and New Testament with Illustrations 1765 Call #220 B47 An63, Research Center, Iowa Historical Society Library and Archives.

129. Hawkeye Heritage, Iowa Genealogical Society Newsletter, #23, Winter 1988, transcribed hand written family records from Joseph Ankeny Bible, Pages 220 to 223.

130. FindAGrave.com, Memorial #35927177, Sarah Irvine Ankeny.

131. Iowa Select Marriages 1809-1992, Ancestry.com.

132. 1880 US Census, Des Moines, Polk, Iowa, Florence Ankeny Russell.

133. Woodland Cemetery, see City of Des Moines, Iowa website.

134. Nicholas Barron Family History 1731-1994, copy provided to Karla Wright from Ruth Barron, May 2014.

135. Heritage of Anna Elizabeth Barron Rigdon, 2014, Karla Rigdon Wright.

136. Iowa: Its History and Its Foremost Citizens, 1918, Johnson Brigham.

137. A Memorial and Biographical Record of Iowa, Illustrated, Volume II, 1896, Page 1154.

138. Des Moines: The Pioneer of Municipal Progress and Reform of the Middle West Together with the History of Polk County Iowa the Largest, Most Populous and Most Prosperous County in the State of Iowa, Johnson Brigham, 1911.

139. 1880 US Census, Quincy, Adams County, Iowa, Fostina and Henry Ankeny.

140. 1870 US Census, Madison Township, Polk County, Iowa, Ellen and Peter Dewalt Ankeny.

141. Iowa: Its History and Its Foremost Citizens, 1918, by Johnson Brigham.

142. 1885 Iowa State Census, Centerville, Appanoose, Iowa, Mary Bird and Benson Israel.

143. FindAGrave.com, Memorial #35927186, John Fletcher Ankeny.

144. FindAGrave.com, Memorial #35927191, Rosina Bonnet Ankeny.

145. Quilt, Ankeny Area Historical Society, Ankeny, Iowa, donated by Ernest and Judy Brown, names on quilt are John Fletcher Ankeny, Harriet Giese Ankeny and Harriet Ankeny Mott.

146. FindAGrave.com, Memorial #37896703, Rose Ankeny Lewis, Historical Journal of the More Family, November 1934.

147. 1910 US Census, Ankona, St Lucie, Florida, Paul Lorah Ankeny.

148. 1910 US Census, Ankona, St Lucie, Florida, Rose Bonnet and Edgar Lewis.

149. 1895 Iowa State Census, Prescott, Adams County, Iowa, Joseph and Elma Rogers.

150. 1900 US Census, Quincy, Adams County, Iowa, Louetta and John Ankeny.

151. Ankeny Family Bibles, 1) New Testament 1835 (contains hand written family records) Call #220 B47 A63; 2) Martin Luther New Testament 1807 Call #220 B47 An61; 3) German Old and New Testament

with Illustrations 1765 Call #220 B47 An63, Research Center, Iowa Historical Society Library and Archives.

152. Souvenir of Des Moines, The Mail and Times, 1891.

153. Ankeny Family Records and Research, 2016, RootsMagic Database, Karla Rigdon Wright.

154. Reticule (drawstring purse), Catalog Number A01663, Iowa Historical Society Library and Archives.

155. FindAGrave.com, Memorial #35927169, Harriet Susanna Giese Ankeny.

156. Obituary for Harriet Susanna Giese Ankeny, Adams County Free Press, Corning, Iowa, April 22, 1897.

157. The Annals of Iowa, Harriett Ankeney, Volume 3, Number 2, 1897, Page 160. (name misspelled in publication)

158. FindAGrave.com, Memorial #80725651, Josephine Chorpenning Barron.

159. Heritage of Anna Elizabeth Barron Rigdon, 2014, Karla Rigdon Wright.

160. History of Franklin County Iowa, I. L. Stuart, 1914. Biographies by Don Turner.

161. The Annals of Iowa, Iowa Historical Building, Volume 4, Number 2, 1899, Pages 81 – 100.

162. Heritage of Anna Elizabeth Barron Rigdon, 2014, Karla Rigdon Wright.

163. Directory of the National Society of the Daughters of the American Revolution, 1901.

164. Abigail Adams Chapter D A R, Des Moines, Iowa.

165. 1900 US Census, Washington, District of Columbia, Harriet Louise Ankeny.

166. Iowa: Its History and Its Foremost Citizens, Volume II, 1918, by Johnson Brigham, pages 52 to 55.

167. FindAGrave.com, Memorial #36550305, John Russell Barcroft.

168. The Annals of Iowa, John Russell Barcroft, Volume 5, Number 1, 1901, Page 80.

169. Iowa: Its History and Its Foremost Citizens, 1918, Johnson Brigham.

170. American Civil War General Officers, Historical Data Systems, Ancestry.com, 1999.

171. US School Catalogs 1765-1935, Page 9, 1853, Western Reserve College, Ohio.

172. US Civil War Soldier Records and Profiles, Illinois: Roster of Officers and Enlisted Men, Heitman: Register of United States Army 1789-1903, National Archives: Index to Federal Pension Records, Dyer: A Compendium of the War of the Rebellion Brevet Brigadier Generals in Blue.

173. S A R, Sons of the American Revolution documentation. Member #10474.

174. A Memorial and Biographical Record of Iowa, Illustrated, Volume II, 1896, Page 1154, General Rollin V. Ankeny.

175. FindAGrave.com, Memorial #17655505, General Rollin Valentine Ankeny.

176. The Annals of Iowa, Rollin V. Ankeny, Volume 5, Number 4, 1902, Page 320.

177. FindAGrave.com, Memorial #35927187, Sarah "Sally" Wolgamot Ankeny.

178. Heritage of Anna Elizabeth Barron Rigdon, 2014, Karla Rigdon Wright.

179. 1900 US Census, 123 East Grand, Des Moines, Polk County, Iowa, Florence Russell and Sally Ankeny and Fletcher Russell.

180. 1910 US Census, Des Moines, Polk County, Iowa, Florence Russell.

181. Henry Giese Ankeny Papers, 1855-1919, MS2008.16, Special Collections, State Historical Society of Iowa, Des Moines, Iowa.

182. Iowa Select Marriages 1809-1992, Ancestry.com.

183. US Headstone Applications for Military Veterans 1925-1963.

184. US Census, 1920, Ankona, St Lucie, Florida, Edyth and Rollin V. Ankeny.

185. Kiss Josey For Me, Collection of Henry Giese Ankeny Civil War Letters, Florence Marie Ankeny Cox, 1974, Page 193.

186. Des Moines: The Pioneer of Municipal Progress and Reform of the Middle West Together with the History of Polk County Iowa the

Largest, Most Populous and Most Prosperous County in the State of Iowa, Johnson Brigham, 1911.

187. Iowa: Its History and Its Foremost Citizens, 1918, by Johnson Brigham.

188. Kiss Josey For Me, Collection of Henry Giese Ankeny Civil War Letters, Florence Marie Ankeny Cox,1974.

189. Henry Giese Ankeny Papers, 1855-1919, MS2008.16, Special Collections, State Historical Society of Iowa, Des Moines, Iowa.

190. US Consular Registration Certificates 1907-1918.

191. FindAGrave.com, Memorial #40596122, Henry Giese Ankeny.

192. D A R, Daughters of the American Revolution documentation, Member #23133.

193. Abigail Adams Chapter D A R, Des Moines, Iowa.

194. Washington Post, article documents Harriet L Ankeny attended President T. Roosevelt White House reception, July 25, 1906.

195. Women's Suffrage in Iowa Online Exhibit, Mary Ankeny Hunter, Iowa's Suffrage Scrapbook - 1920 and Beyond - Iowa Women's Archives - the University of Iowa Libraries.

196. Iowa Women's Archives, University of Iowa., Guide to the Mary Ankeny Hunter Memoir, 1940, Iowa Women's Archives, Collection Number IWA0097, University of Iowa Libraries.

197. The Annals of Iowa, Fred H. Hunter, Volume 25, Number 2, Fall 1943, Page 141.

198. Des Moines: The Pioneer of Municipal Progress and Reform of the Middle West Together with the History of Polk County Iowa the Largest, Most Populous and Most Prosperous County in the State of Iowa, Johnson Brigham, 1911, pages 626 to 634.

199. Parasol, Catalog Number 08764, Iowa Historical Society Library and Archives.

200. Reticule (drawstring purse) Catalog Number A01663, Iowa Historical Society Library and Archives.

201. History of Franklin County Iowa, I. L. Stuart, 1914, Biographies by Don Turner.

202. Des Moines Iowa Oral History Project, Des Moines Public Library, Interview with Robert Brown Ankeny, Audio Recording, 1975.

203. Wikipedia.org, Villisca, Iowa Axe Murders, 1912.

204. FindAGrave.com, Memorial #14861990, Henry H Clark.

205. The World Book Encyclopedia, 1986 Edition, G, Page 179, Frank and Lillian Gilbreth – Pioneers of Scientific Management.

206. FindAGrave.com, Memorial #56988567, Mabel Ankeny Matthews.

207. US Census, 1910, Des Moines Ward 5, Polk County, Iowa, Mary Louise and George Burnett.

208. US Census, 1910, Des Moines, Polk County, Iowa, Daisy and Frank Green.

209. US Census, 1910, Ankona, Saint Lucie County, Florida, Rose Bonnet and Edgar Lewis.

210. Des Moines: The Pioneer of Municipal Progress and Reform of the Middle West Together with the History of Polk County Iowa the Largest, Most Populous and Most Prosperous County in the State of Iowa, Johnson Brigham, 1911.

211. US Mexican War Pension Index, Peter D Ankeny, Washington D.C.

212. US School Catalogs 1765-1935, Kenyon College, 1853, Peter Dewalt Ankeny.

213. FindAGrave.com, Memorial #25229527, Peter Dewalt Ankeny.

214. State Historical Society of Iowa, Archives and Library and Museum, 600 E Locust St, Des Moines, Iowa.

215. FindAGrave.com, Memorial #36550315, Susan Ankeny Barcroft.

216. Des Moines, Iowa Oral History Project, Des Moines Public Library, Interview with Robert Brown Ankeny, Audio Recording, 1975.

217. Des Moines, Iowa Oral History Project, Des Moines Public Library, Interview with Robert Brown Ankeny, Audio Recording, 1975.

218. Green Hills - An Album of Iowa State Memories, page 50.

219. The World Book Encyclopedia, 1986 Edition, W, Page 322, Woman Suffrage.

220. The World Book Encyclopedia, 1986 Edition, H, Page 60, Warren Harding.

221. FindAGrave.com, Memorial #35927175, Harriet Louise Ankeny.

Made in the USA
Middletown, DE
21 July 2016